# MEGAN HART 5/14

## SARAH MORGAN

*tangled up*

COSMO RED-HOT READS
FROM HARLEQUIN

Recycling programs
for this product may
not exist in your area.

ISBN-13: 978-0-373-62244-3

TANGLED UP

Copyright © 2014 by Harlequin Books S.A.

The publisher acknowledges the copyright holders of the individual works as follows:

CROSSING THE LINE
Copyright © 2014 by Megan Hart

BURNED
Copyright © 2014 by Sarah Morgan

For questions and comments about the quality of this book, please contact us at
CustomerService@Harlequin.com.

Printed in U.S.A.

# CONTENTS

## About the Author

**Megan Hart** is the award-winning and multipublished author of more than thirty novels, novellas and short stories. Her work has been published in almost every genre, including contemporary women's fiction, historical romance, romantic suspense and erotica. Megan lives in the deep, dark woods of Pennsylvania with her husband and children, and is currently working on her next novel for Harlequin MIRA. You can contact Megan through her website at www.meganhart.com.

## Books by Megan Hart

### Cosmo Red-Hot Reads from Harlequin

LETTING GO (November 2014 as an ebook)
LETTING GO will also be in the anthology CAPTIVATED,
  on sale in print November 2014.

### Harlequin MIRA

BROKEN
DEEPER
DIRTY
PRECIOUS AND FRAGILE THINGS
THE FAVOR
SWITCH
TEMPTED

Dear Reader,

RED-HOT READ!

That says it all, doesn't it? I'm thrilled to be a part of the Cosmo Red-Hot Reads from Harlequin publishing program, bringing short, sexy fiction to readers who want their red-hot reads.

My heroine, Caite Fox, is just the sort of woman who'd like to get her hands on a red-hot read of her own—if she had time to do any reading for pleasure, that is. She's kept pretty busy chasing after her boss, Jameson Wolfe, as they both try to wrangle a pair of out-of-control clients in their media management business. She's the kind of woman who knows how to get what she wants, though, and she wants more than just the corner office.

She wants Jameson.

And he's going to let her have him, even if he doesn't know it in the beginning, because the sly Miss Fox has everything the big bad Wolfe craves. Smart, sexy, with a great sense of humor, she's the kind of woman he's been dreaming about getting on his knees for. Literally.

As both of them discover each other, I hope readers will fall in love with them as I have along the way!

Thanks for reading!

M

# CROSSING THE LINE

## Megan Hart

# 1

JAMISON WOLFE WAS shouting again.

He did that a lot. On the phone, mostly, though Caite had heard him hollering in the lobby a few times when some particularly aggressive paparazzi had managed to get past the building security and find their way to the Wolfe and Baron offices in pursuit of a few of the company's clients. Jamison lived up to his name when that happened, snarling and growling in defense of those he considered to be under his protection.

It was totally hot.

So far, Caite Fox had avoided being the recipient of Jamison's fury, though she'd often thought about poking him to see if she could taunt him into losing control. The thought of it had been the subject of more than a few late-night fantasies, but she hadn't done anything about it. First of all, teasing your boss into a hatefuck, no matter how exciting it seemed, was definitely a bad idea no matter where you worked. Second, it was super hard to seduce a guy who barely seemed to notice you existed. She worked mostly with Elise, scarcely saying more than a word to Jamison, despite her constant sur-

veillance of him. So she bit her tongue and focused on staying under Jamison's rage radar, doing her work the best she
could—which was pretty damned well. She could say that and
not be bragging. She'd been with Wolfe and Baron for only
eight months but had already managed to accumulate an impressive client list of her own even while working on everything else her two bosses had delegated to her. This was the
best job she'd ever had. Great perks, decent salary.

She considered the chance to surreptitiously ogle Jamison
Wolfe one of the perks, and since he barely gave her the time
of day, she had a lot of chances to check him out without
him noticing. Now the rough, deep rumble of his voice rose
through the office walls and sent a shiver creeping deliciously
through her, and for a moment, Caite sat back in her chair to
see if she could catch a peek at him across the hall. He often
paced while he hollered, and she wasn't disappointed now
when he passed by his open door. Today he wore the charcoal
suit with the deep pink shirt and silver-and-pink tie. One of
Caite's favorites.

Jamison pivoted on one perfectly shined black shoe, running
a hand through his dark hair and rumpling it as she watched.
When he turned, the light caught the glint of silver at his temples. With the phone clamped to his ear, his brow furrowed,
he looked both formidable and regal, even when he started
shouting again. That was the thing about him. Unlike a lot
of men, who sputtered or turned red-faced and ugly in their
fury, Jamison Wolfe never looked anything less than perfect.

"Caite?"

Startled, Caite swiveled in her chair to fully face the door,
where her other boss, Elise Baron, had appeared. In contrast to Jamison, Elise looked anything but perfect. Her fair
hair, usually pulled into a sleek French twist, had come loose
around her face with pieces stuck lightly to her glistening fore-

head and cheeks. In the past month, her pregnancy had really begun to show, and her maternity suit wasn't as tailored or flattering as the ones she usually wore—now her blouse had come untucked from the elastic waistband of her skirt. She'd taken off her shoes to reveal swollen feet and ankles, and her pale skin looked not only threaded with blue and red varicose veins but also oddly dimpled, as though she'd poked a finger into rising bread dough and left behind an indentation that was only slowly filling in.

"Elise. Hey. Are you okay?"

"No. I don't think so." Elise swallowed heavily and gripped the doorframe as she swayed. "I don't feel well at all."

"Sit." Caite was up at once, taking Elise by the elbow to lead her to the futon across from her desk. Elise gave a grateful sigh as she sank onto it. "What's going on?"

"I woke up with a headache today, but I figured it was just my normal sinus stuff going on. Allergies. But it's been getting worse and I'm noticing a lot of swelling in my ankles." Elise blinked rapidly, her normally implacable demeanor shaken. "I should call Steph."

"You sit. I'll do it. I think I should call your doctor, too. You don't look good." Caite knelt in front of Elise to chafe her hands. Elise's cheeks, plump with pregnancy, nevertheless looked hollowed, her skin gray and clammy. Caite didn't know much about pregnancy beyond the fact she had no desire to get in that condition herself for a long time, but something was clearly not right. "Let me get you some water, too."

With a nod, Elise sat back against the futon's rigid cushion and closed her eyes. Caite got up and went to the water cooler in the hall. She drew a paper cup of cool water and paused in Jamison's doorway on the way back, but he was still on the phone facing away from her. He'd moved beyond the yelling to the coldly determined negotiating portion of the conversation, which meant he was almost finished. Poking her head around the corner to the reception area, Caite motioned to Bobby, who was busy at the front desk dealing with the mail.

"Hey. Get Steph on the line, Elise isn't feeling well. Get the number of her doctor, too. I'm going to go back and sit with her, make sure she's okay. She looked really bad."

Bobby looked surprised. "What's wrong with her?"

"Don't know. Phone, Bobby," Caite said firmly. For a guy who worked for a company that dealt in handling the media affairs of celebrities, he hadn't yet mastered the art of not being nosy.

She took the water to Elise, who didn't look any better but sipped slowly from the cup. Caite looked her over, cataloging the symptoms she could see so that when she got the doctor on the phone, she'd be ready to describe them. The phone on her desk rang with the distinctive one-two beat of an internal transfer. That would be Steph.

"Hey," she said, wasting no time with a greeting. "It's Caite. Elise isn't feeling well. She asked me to call you."

Steph reacted immediately. "What's wrong? Is she sick? Oh, God. Is it the baby? Is the baby coming early?"

"I don't think so." Caite quickly described the symptoms she'd noted, listening to the rapid sound of Steph's breathing. She was going to hyperventilate at this rate. "Did you give Bobby the doctor's number?"

"Yes. Oh, God. It sounds like it's preeclampsia. I told her not to go into work today!"

"It's going to be all right." Caite looked over at Elise, whose color was slightly better, but nothing else seemed to have changed. "Do you want to talk to her?"

Elise opened her eyes then and shook her head with a small smile. "Bathroom," she mouthed.

"Steph, she went to the bathroom. Listen, when…Hold on.

Bobby's putting a call through." Caite transferred to the other line, where she ran through the symptoms again with the doctor, who determined that it did indeed sound as if Elise was suffering from preeclampsia and who told Caite she needed to be brought into the hospital immediately.

After handing the phone to Elise so she could speak with the doctor, Caite ducked back to reception, where Bobby was busy dealing with an increasingly hysterical Steph. He was good at this aspect of his job, and he handled Elise's wife with easy efficiency. Fortunately, none of them had any scheduled appointments yet this morning, and the reception waiting area was empty.

"She's going to come here," Bobby said with a hand over the mouthpiece.

"No," Caite countered. "Tell her to meet us at the hospital."

She could hear Steph's shriek of dismay all the way from across the room, but there wasn't any time to deal with that. Caite went back to rap on Jamison's door. He still had the phone pressed to his ear and gave her an irritated wave, dismissing her. Not sure how important it was to interrupt him at this point anyway—it wasn't as if the doc were calling for an ambulance or anything, right?—Caite went back to her own office to find Elise on her feet. Unsteady, still pale, but looking determined.

"I need to get my stuff."

"I'll have Bobby call us a cab." Caite put out a hand to help keep Elise on her feet. "It's going to be all right."

Elise nodded, mouth wobbling as she managed to find a small false smile. "I hope so."

Caite had no idea if everything was going to be okay or not, but one thing she was really good at was holding the hands, both literally and figuratively, of nervous people. She took Elise's hand now and squeezed. "It will be okay. You'll see."

★ ★ ★

Part of the reason Jamison liked working with Brett Denni-
son over at Ace Talent was that the other man knew when to
stop negotiating. Not that Jamison didn't love digging down
deep to figure out the right angles for the contract and getting
the other guy to agree to what was best for Wolfe and Baron
and nobody else. Jamison liked the power of getting someone
to do what he wanted them to do…but there was also that
perfect, sweet moment when the other person at last capitu-
lated, and everything could move on from there.

"I'll have Caite work up the final agreements and send
them over," Jamison said now. "Good to be working with
you again, Brett."

Brett laughed. "Yeah, yeah, that's what you say when you're
riding in that Beemer on my dime."

"It's not your dime," Jamison said, not bothering to point
out that he did not, and never would, drive a BMW. Jamison
had a '64 Mustang that had been his old man's. Completely
restored. "It's the blood, sweat and tears of your clients."

"Fair enough. Lunch next week?"

"Call Bobby. He'll set it up."

With the pleasantries out of the way, both men disconnected. Jamison sat back in his chair, finally, to put his feet up
on the desk and take a breath. He'd been so caught up in his
negotiation with Brett that he hadn't been paying much attention to the passing of time, but damn, the office had gone
quiet. The blinking light on his desk phone told him he had
messages waiting, but he didn't bother to check them. Anyone he really wanted to talk to had his cell number; anyone
calling him on the office line was going to have to wait until
he felt like checking in.

His stomach rumbled, and the hunger he'd been fending
off since lunch, when he'd taken the time only to grab a pro-

tein bar, roared into full life. The headache followed after, poking at his temples like a dozen tiny devils dancing. With a muttered invective, Jamison pulled open his desk drawer to grab another protein bar, but the bin held only dust and disappointment.

"Dammit." He got to his feet and went to the front desk, where Bobby usually kept a basket of candy, but a few mints weren't going to do the trick.

Where the hell was everyone? Bobby might've been out the door on the dot of five, but Elise and Caite certainly should've still been finishing up some work. Elise especially, since her plan was to get as much done as she could before she went on maternity leave. She'd planned to work from home for the first couple of months but even so needed to get everything settled before then. Caite, on the other hand…Jamison frowned. The girl had worked in the office for all of a few months, not long enough to start slacking off, in his opinion. And dammit, there wasn't even any hot coffee in the pot Bobby was supposed to keep fresh for waiting clients. Grumbling, Jamison strode back to his office to shut everything down before he headed out.

He'd missed the ding of the elevator door opening but looked up as the scent of pizza wafted toward him. Not pizza. Stromboli, the best kind, from Gino's down the street. He found Caite in the conference room, setting out the familiar cardboard takeout box, along with a couple of paper plates and napkins. A six pack of Tröegs Pale Ale, too. She looked up when he came in.

"Hey."

Jamison paused in the doorway. "I thought everyone was gone for the night."

Caite straightened and put a hand on one hip, her head tilting to study him for a second, lips pursed. "And you were pissed off, huh?"

"No." Well, he had been, hadn't he? At least a little. "Okay, annoyed."

She laughed, shaking her head. "You have no idea, do you?"

"About what? That everyone else around here seems to think that it's okay to skip off, whatever, just because the clock says it's time?" He frowned at her, trying to remember what they'd gone over in her initial interview, but Elise had handled most of that. "I thought we made it clear when we took you on that this wasn't going to be a nine-to-fiver."

"For your information, Mr. Wolfe," Caite said coolly, going back to setting out the food, "I was a little busy this afternoon, helping Elise."

"And that's an excuse?" The words spilled out of him, tasting irrational, and he knew it, but still a little high from his fierce negotiations with Brett, Jamison was having a little trouble coming back to the world of getting along with other people.

"You skipped lunch today, didn't you."

Jamison frowned harder. "What the hell does that have to do with anything?"

"I had to take Elise to the hospital because she was having preeclampsia and possibly going into an early labor," Caite said, voice hard, "which you'd have known if you paid any attention to what goes on in here aside from ragging on people for not living up to your kind of asinine expectations. But if you'd eaten lunch today, I bet you'd have at least asked me what was going on before you launched into a tirade about my lack of work ethic, so sit down and eat something before *your* blood pressure gets too high."

He froze. "Elise? What? Is she all right? What the hell? Why didn't someone—?"

"Sit. Down," Caite commanded in a tone that sliced right through him. "Now."

Jamison sat.

They stared at each other for a moment before she pushed a plate of stromboli toward him. "Eat."

He dug in, tearing off a hunk of soft bread and gooey cheese and chewing rapidly before taking another bite. He was starving, and she was right. He was an asshole when he was hungry. But that didn't mean he didn't care about his partner.

"She's fine," Caite said before he could ask her anything else. She picked daintily at her own stromboli, cutting it neatly with her fork and knife and letting it cool before taking a bite. "They put her on some meds and are monitoring her overnight. Steph's with her. But they're not sure when she'll be back to work. Definitely not tomorrow, anyway."

"Tomorrow's the big meeting with that bunch of yahoos from that reality show. The one about the house." Jamison reached for a beer and passed her one. He cracked the top and took a gulp, relishing the crisp flavor of the ale. "Elise was point person on that one. She knows how I feel about working with those types."

"Those types," Caite said, "are willing to pay a lot of money for our services."

Jamison paused, stromboli halfway to his mouth. He set it down. "Do I detect a note of disapproval, Ms. Fox?"

"Just truth." Caite gave him another one of those assessing looks. "They'll bring Wolfe and Baron a lot of attention, too. It's why Elise took them on."

"And she was supposed to deal with them. I'm the guy who dots the i's and crosses the t's. She's the one who deals with the clients." After the words came out, he realized he sounded unsympathetic and kind of like a dick.

Caite cracked the top off a beer for herself and tipped it toward him. "She was worried about how you'd handle it, to be honest."

"Dammit." That didn't sit well with him, not at all. "But she's going to be okay, right?"

It must've been the right thing to say, because instead of frowning, Caite gave him another slow grin. And good god-damn, that girl could smile. It lit her entire face, and Jamison couldn't understand how he'd never noticed it until just now. Maybe because this was the first time since the initial interview that he'd actually spent more than a couple minutes talking to her. It had been Elise's idea to hire her, and Jamison hadn't paid much attention beyond signing the extra paycheck.

"She'll be okay." Caite gave a firm nod, then looked hesitant for the first time tonight. "I have to believe that, anyway. Power of positive thinking."

That didn't make him feel better. "Should I call her?"

"Not anymore tonight. Steph was going to stay with her and promised she'd call with an update in the morning. She'll be okay," Caite repeated, sounding more convinced this time. "Finish your dinner, Jamison."

He was already feeling better after having consumed just half the piece she'd given him, and he settled back in his chair with the beer. "Can we reschedule?"

"We don't have to. I'll take it on."

He sipped the beer for a moment, thinking about the new clients. He'd argued with Elise about taking them on, money or no, because if there was one thing Jamison didn't want Wolfe and Baron turning into, it was a babysitting service for douche bags. She'd fought him on it for a few reasons, money one of them. Never enough money, she'd told him, not with a baby on the way and the economy the way it was. The other reason was even simpler—the trio of reality TV stars might be famous only for their stupidity, recklessness and lack of couth, but they were super fucking famous. The biggest-name clients Wolfe and Baron had scored to date.

"You don't have the experience," he told Caite flatly. "I'm going to have to head this one."

She sighed and rolled her eyes, not even trying to hide it. Jamison blinked, surprised by both her reaction…and his lack of it. He'd fired people for less than that. A whole bunch of them as a matter of fact, which was why he and Elise and Bobby were the only ones working in this place, at least until she'd insisted on hiring Caite. But with a full belly and the beer, his favorite, mellowing him a little, all he did was grunt.

"You're going to give yourself an ulcer," Caite said.

Jamison took another long pull of beer. "You have a better idea?"

"I told you my better idea."

"You've been here, what, six months?"

"Nearly eight," Caite said with another shake of her head that left him feeling uncomfortably ashamed.

"And you think you have what it takes?"

"I've been handling clients on my own for the past four months," Caite said quietly. "Brought some in on my own, too."

Which he ought to have known. Dammit. He'd been so caught up in his own client list that he'd been letting Elise deal with the "new hire," who, as it turned out, wasn't all that new any longer. "I thought we took you on as an assistant. Filing. Copying."

"Fetching coffee?" Caite gave him another one of those stunning grins. "Relax. I've been doing all that, too. But technically, you took me on as a junior account manager. Not an assistant."

"Elise assigned you other work, huh?" Jamison finished his beer and set the empty bottle on the table. Caite nodded. "She's a little nicer than I am."

"More than a little," came the answer.

Again, from anyone else, the smart-ass reaction would've probably sent him into a fury, but something about this girl… This woman, he corrected himself. Because Caite was young but not girlish. Not at all. Something about this woman eased him away from anger. Like taking in a breath of cool air when you'd spent too long in a sauna.

"She must think highly of you," Jamison said.

"I think she's been pleased with my work. You'd be pleased, too, if you'd paid attention to it." Caite sipped her beer and gave him a long look over the top of it. "You should pay better attention, Jamison."

Something slithered through him then, at that tone. Those words. The calmly assessing look in her blue, blue eyes. Her confidence…and that smile.

"Tell you what," he said, leaning closer. "If you can prove you can handle it, I'll let you work on this project."

"Oh, I can handle it," Caite said. "The question is, can you?"

# 2

"YOU'RE A LITTLE cocky, aren't you?" Jamison said with a gleam in his dark eyes that had Caite sitting up a little straighter to meet his gaze head-on.

"Pot, have you met kettle?"

To her relief, because it could've gone either way, he laughed. Then tipped his empty bottle at her before tossing it into the recycling bin next to the conference room door. "You're in for a helluva lot of work. It's not just setting up a media plan for them, you know. They're all already on all the sites—"

"I know," Caite cut in smoothly, thinking of the after-hours work she'd already put in pulling together a media management plan for the three new clients. "It's not just monitoring their activity but doing damage control, as well as coordinating coverage when they're booked for gigs and managing that, too. Getting them sponsorships. Stuff like that. I'm not a total newbie. Before I came to work here, I had three years in social media experience."

Jamison snorted laughter. "You probably don't remember a time when social media didn't exist."

"I'm almost thirty years old, Jamison. I can assure you, I remember a life before Connex."

He looked thoughtful. "It's not going to be easy. These kids are hard to handle."

"Which is why we got them to pay us the big bucks. Nobody else wants them, not even for the notoriety."

For a moment, she wished she hadn't said that, even though it was the truth. Wolfe and Baron were not notorious, and there was a reason for that. Jamison had started this business with an eye for clients who traveled in influential circles but didn't make a scene. Businessmen, politicians, the occasional socialite. Once Elise had come on board, Wolfe and Baron had begun to expand into the celebrity arena but still handled mostly theater actors, artists, classical musicians, not rock stars. Handling these three reality TV stars was totally new ground for them, but Elise had been adamant about taking them on.

Nellie Bower, Paxton France and Tommy Sanders were going to put Wolfe and Baron on the map.

And Caite intended to be part of that. She eyed Jamison now. "I can handle them."

Jamison narrowed his eyes. "What makes you think so?"

"Because I'm good at what I do. I told you. Because I think outside the box. Because I'm young and hip." She paused with a smile. "Because I've actually watched *Treasure House,* unlike you."

"Piece-of-shit show."

"Oh, it's a shit show, all right, which is why it gets the ratings, and why those three are so popular right now." Caite shrugged. "Look, it's no *Doctor Who,* but there've been some decent episodes."

"You watch *Doctor Who?*"

Should she be offended at his surprise? "Um, duh. Yes."

"I used to love that show as a kid."

"Well, here's some news for you, Gramps—it's been updated since then."

He looked startled at first, then gave her a grudging laugh that sent a thrill all through her. A laugh from her curmudgeonly boss was as rare as icicles in a Texas July. "Some people have lives, Ms. Fox. Like we do things other than watch television."

Somehow she doubted that he had much of a life. It was all work with him. Hours in the office, hours outside the office. She didn't know much about his personal life, other than that he had no wife, no kids and seemingly no family. Maybe he'd sprung full-grown from a trumpet, like in that old Greek myth she could never remember—and that would make sense, because he sure had the body of a Greek god.

*Hold it in, girl,* she counseled herself. *He's your boss and a little too bossy for you even if he didn't sign your paycheck.*

"I have a *life,*" she said instead, like a challenge.

He took it. She'd known he would. It was in the glint of his eyes and lift of his chin and something in the way his breath shifted. She'd watched him go head-to-head with too many people not to know what sorts of things got him going, but had she deliberately chosen this tone of voice, those words? Caite thought that maybe she had.

"Oh, yeah?"

"Yeah," she said in a lower voice, meeting his eyes without looking away. "A rich, full life that includes time for television, along with lots of other…things."

Jamison pinned her with his gaze, his teeth bared a little in a predatory smile. "And you think I don't have a rich, full life? Why? Because I don't rot my brain with shitty reality television shows?"

"No," she said on a low breath. "Because you don't make time for those other things."

For a moment, she thought he'd reach across the table and take her by the chin. Or, oh, God, fist his fingers in her hair. But of course he didn't, and wouldn't, even if he was suddenly looking at her as though she were Little Red Riding Hood and he a different sort of wolf. Still, the look made Caite shift in her seat, squeezing her thighs together, watching him look her over.

"Like what other things?" Jamison asked.

"When's the last time you went dancing, for example?"

He frowned. "I don't like to dance."

She laughed. "I'm not surprised."

For a moment, it was his turn to look offended. "What makes you say that?"

"You're not patient enough to be a good dancer."

"The hell does that mean?" His frown didn't break his face the way it would've on another man. It only emphasized his intense good looks. "Not patient enough?"

Caite shrugged. "It means that even though you're athletic and in good shape, you don't have the patience to learn any sort of coordinated dancing. And freestyle would annoy you, trying to keep up with someone who wasn't zigging left when you wanted to go right. You'd need a partner who understood you better than you know yourself in order to keep up with you."

His mouth opened as though he meant to speak, but Caite kept up before he could.

"You don't like crowds with loud music, and though you like to drink, you don't like being around people who are out-of-control drunk. That's why you don't like the new clients, isn't it? At least part of it?"

"They're disgusting," Jamison muttered, cutting his gaze from hers. He wiped at his mouth with his fingertips before looking back at her. "You seem to think you know an awful lot about me."

"Sorry if I overstepped," she said, not sorry at all.

Jamison wet his lips with the tip of his tongue. "You really think you can handle those three?"

"Yes. I really do." Confidence was everything; Caite had learned that a long time ago. She smiled at him, hoping to get at least the hint of a grin in return, but Jamison only stared at her steadily. For a long time.

He broke first, finally. "Fine. You're on it."

"Hooray!" Caite cried.

He looked taken aback, then shook his head and sighed. "Hooray."

"C'mon. Say it like you mean it," Caite said, standing and leaning over the table to put her hands flat on it so she could look him in the eyes. She only meant to tease him—Jamison Wolfe had long impressed her as the sort of man who needed to be teased now and then. But at the way his eyes narrowed and mouth thinned, Caite worried she'd gone a little too far.

Then, watching him watch her, she began to hope she had.

"I'll be able to call in every day." Elise, looking tired, plucked at the comforter with a surreptitious look toward the bedroom door, where Steph was likely hovering. She gave Jamison a small smile. "And I'll have my laptop. I can handle some stuff from here."

"You should just take it easy." Jamison settled on the edge of the bed to pat her hand, then had a second thought and twined her fingers in his. He and Elise had been friends since high school, had spent more than a few nights tangled up in the same blankets. Never lovers, always friends, they'd shared probably every dark secret each had ever had. He knew better than anyone how unbreakable she was. And still, looking at

her now, so pale and somehow shrunken despite the discon-
certingly enormous mound of her belly under the blankets, all
he could think about was how close he might be to losing her.

"She'll be taking it easy." Steph peeked around the doorway. "If I have to tie her to the bed, she'll be taking it easy."

"Kinky," Elise murmured with a loving smile toward her
wife that lit her eyes but didn't do much to put color back in
her cheeks.

"Too much information." Jamison squeezed Elise's fingers
and stood. "I'm going to head back to the office. I'm glad
you're feeling better, and you take care of yourself. Stay in
bed, do what the doctor tells you, you hear me?"

"Jamison, hang on. Stay a minute. Steph, baby, can you
bring me some hot tea?" When the other woman had gone,
Elise turned to him. "You and Caite have the new clients
covered, yes?"

He hesitated, thinking about the conversation he'd had yes-
terday evening with the wily Ms. Fox. "She says she's good
to take them over."

"You're going to have to let her. We hired her for a reason, you know."

"You're the one who told me the triplets of destruction were
going to be our name makers. And you want me to leave them
in the hands of our junior office assistant?"

Elise laughed. Hard. "She's a junior account manager, and
she's been taking on client work since a few months after she
started. Caite has a good strong PR background, first of all.
And social media savvy. Which is supposed to be our thing,
you know. Remember?"

"I remember." He'd always been much better at the background aspects of the business. Getting clients and keeping
them. Negotiating. Not the day-to-day handling of them, or

even of the office itself. That was Elise's expertise, and now, he guessed, Caite's.

Elise looked at him. "You can't handle everything alone, Jamison. You're going to have to let her do her job."

"And if she totally screws up? What then?"

"She won't." Elise held up a hand to keep him from saying more. "But if she does, look…those crazy kids have their own mess already. It's not like we could make anything worse for them. If anything, we should pray they screw up, big-time, and soon, so we can actually work to redeem them."

"You're good at that." He laughed, thinking of a lot of the things with clients that had happened over the years. Press releases in the beginning, carefully crafted statements of apology. More recently, well-timed tweets or Connex updates.

"You need to relax." She eyed him. "You don't want to be the next one to end up in the hospital bed."

For a moment, he thought about laughing off her concern, but then he shook his head. Elise had been there with him when his dad died, too young, of a stroke and heart attack brought on by a lifetime of unhealthy habits. "I take care of myself."

"Sure. You run, you watch what you eat to the point where I wonder if you even like food. But you don't take care of yourself, honey." She paused. "I worry about you."

"You shouldn't." Her words sent a flash of heat through him. Embarrassment more than comfort. They'd been friends for a long time, and she could look right inside him, down to his core, but that didn't mean it ever felt easier to be seen that way. Jamison liked his walls high, strong and topped with iron spikes.

"Well, you can't stop me. Now get out of here before Steph chases you out with a broom. Dinner next week?"

"Yeah. Here, I presume." He grinned, ducking away from the pillow she tossed at him. "I'll bring something good."

"You'd better." She sighed as the door creaked open and Steph appeared with a tray laden with tea and goodies. "Even though it looks like I'm going to be thoroughly spoiled as it is. Thank you, baby."

He turned away as they kissed, another tickle of heat creeping up the back of his neck at the display of affection. It wasn't that he was...jealous, he thought as he ducked out of the room and headed for his car. Relationships were more work than they were worth. He'd had a few girlfriends over the years, and every one of them had turned out to be jealous, greedy and, eventually, demanding. Even the ones who'd claimed they were only interested in something casual. Which said too much about his taste in women, he admitted as he drove back toward the office. Women were a lot of work, and he wasn't the sort to be lonely, so why, then, did the memory of the sparkle in Elise's eyes when she looked at her wife leave him with such an ashen taste in his mouth?

# 3

BOBBY, PUSHING HIS glasses up on his nose, looked up as Jamison got off the elevator. "Mr. Wolfe. You have several messages, and—"

As if on cue, Jamison's phone trilled from his pocket. He noted the name of the caller and sent it to voice mail. He waved at Bobby dismissively and kept going. He had stuff to take care of first. Messages could wait.

"And Ms. Fox is in the conference room with the clients from *Treasure House*," Bobby called after him.

Jamison stopped in his tracks, spinning on one heel. "Huh? They're here?"

"In the conference room," Bobby repeated, standing to point down the hall.

As if Jamison didn't know where the conference room was.

Before Jamison could sneak into his office, the conference room door opened, and Caite poked her head out. Her face lit when she saw him; the grin that spread from ear to ear was bright and delighted. She gestured.

"Jamison! Hi. I'm glad you're here. C'mon in and meet the *Treasure House* clients."

It was the last thing he wanted to do, even though meeting all their new clients was something he always did. With an inward sigh and an outwardly neutral expression, he stalked down the hall. Caite squeezed his elbow as he pushed past her.

"Deep breath," she murmured without losing a bit of her smile. "Their management is paying us triple the highest rate we're currently charging, and we've already been mentioned on three of the top five gossip sites. The phone's been ringing off the hook all day."

He glanced at her. "Since when was it triple?"

"Since I had a little talk with their manager," Caite said as her smile widened and she made a sweeping gesture to encompass the three people seated at the other end of the conference room table. "Jamison Wolfe, I'd like to introduce you to our newest members of the Wolfe and Baron family."

*Here we go,* Jamison thought. *The shit show has begun.*

Nellie Bower and Paxton France had been vociferously denying any sort of romantic relationship, but watching them canoodle on the opposite side of the conference table, Caite knew the pair were shagging like 1970s rec room carpet. Tommy Sanders didn't seem at all fazed by the way Nellie reached to pluck bits of imaginary lint off of Paxton's broad shoulders, which meant he also knew the two were involved. Not that it would've been easy to ignore, since the three of them had been teamed up for the past two years, contractually obligated to be together both in and out of the house in which a multimillion-dollar prize was hidden. This was the show's second season, and the stakes had risen from 3 to 5 million. If the three of them could last until the end of the season and sign on for another, the prize would rise to $7 million.

But it wasn't Caite's job to keep them together. Or break them up, for that matter. Her job was to spin the exploits of these three into something the public would eagerly consume, no matter how stupid they acted. Or how boring. Using her social media management skills, her task would be to keep them in the public eye without oversaturating the market, as well as make sure that everything they did met the corporate sponsors' approval.

She loved it already.

"So. Guys," she said, pinpointing her gaze on Nellie and Pax, who were ignoring her totally for a whispered conversation full of sibilance. Tommy, however, looked at her with the same deadpan stare he'd become famous for. "Let's talk about this week's schedule. You're off from the house this weekend, right?"

The team got weekends free to leave the treasure house and live in the real world while the crew reset the booby traps and clues they'd have to fight and find in the next week's filming. Pax bore a distinct set of fading bruises on his dark cheek that Caite had already seen covered in a blast of comments on the show's Connex fan page, though Pax himself had been smart enough not to breach his contract by mentioning what had caused them in anything he'd said. That had only fueled the fire of commentary as fans tried to figure out what had happened, how close to dying he'd come, the extent of injuries they couldn't see. It had been ratings genius, though Caite suspected it was mostly unplanned on his part. She was having a hard time believing Pax was smart enough to have planned that strategy.

"Yeah." The answer finally came from Tommy, who gave his teammates a small roll of his eyes. "We got the weekend off. Gotta go back in Sunday night."

"So tonight it's parrrrty!" Nellie bounced in her seat and clapped her hands like a toddler promised a pony ride. Her long black hair, dyed beneath with blue and green stripes, flipped over her shoulders. "I'm'a get shit hammered!"

"There's a shocker," Tommy muttered.

From his seat, the formerly silent Jamison said, "Contractually, the three of you have to stay together at all times, right? During filming and not."

"Yeah." Pax nodded and sidled a tiny bit closer to Nellie, though it was obvious he was trying to make it look accidental. "All three of us. All the time. The Three Musketeers."

"More like a PayDay," Tommy said.

Caite grinned at his clever twist on the names of two candy bars. "I guess it's a good thing you like each other, then."

Another one of those sly glances from Pax to Nellie. Caite didn't miss it. Jamison didn't, either. He and Caite shared a look of their own across the table.

"So," Jamison said suddenly. "Where are we going tonight?"

"Your face is gonna stay that way." Caite had sidled up next to Jamison, who stood along the railing overlooking the dance floor where Nellie, Paxton and Tommy were currently taking pictures and signing autographs for their admirers. She'd arranged for the club to advertise their appearance. She didn't look at Jamison but kept her gaze carefully on their three clients. She nudged him gently with an elbow.

He half turned to look at her. "Don't they ever quit?"

"If you had to stay locked in a house full of booby traps, your every move being filmed, for five days out of seven… wouldn't you want to go a little wild when you had a chance for some time off?"

He shook his head. "Hell, no. I'd want to get a good night's sleep."

"You," Caite said, turning to him finally, "could stand to loosen up a little."

Jamison stared her down, but she didn't look away. "You think so, huh."

"I do."

For an instant, just the barest, briefest second, a hint of a smile ghosted along his mouth. It was gone before she could return it. But she'd seen it. There was that.

"You don't have to be here, you know. It's not required. I can handle it." Caite bounced a little on her toes to the beat of the music as she gave a discreet gesture toward their clients. She pulled out her phone to tap in an updated Connex status for the three, sending out another media blip. "We're not babysitters."

Jamison made no move to leave. "When you get them trending in the local radius, then I'll leave."

Caite's brows rose, but she held up her phone to show him the screen of her tracking app. It logged the trending topics in several of the social media apps Wolfe and Baron preferred to utilize and was updated every fifteen minutes. "We're in the top ten on most of them, except for the video ones. We had a brief surge on Buffvid, but that was it."

"Guess you'd better get them posting some video, then, huh?" He gave her a sharklike grin.

It didn't intimidate her.

"You got it," Caite said, then paused to give him a slowly quirking smile designed to get under his skin just a little. "Boss."

She ducked through the crowd to get close to Tommy, who looked happy to see her. At least, he put his arm around her and drew her close as though they were longtime besties instead of just-met acquaintances. Caite didn't mind. Tommy was delicious, long and lean and tattooed. He smelled good, too. He leaned close to talk into her ear.

"Hey, you."

"Can you Buzzvid a couple clips?" She looked past him to where Nellie and Paxton were holding court, happily taking pictures with fans who were hopefully using the right hashtags.

Tommy frowned for a second. "Yeah. Sure. Get in here with me."

He took a shot of the crowd, then of the two of them, with Caite woo-wooing appropriately. She waited for him to send the clip out into the world, then rebuzzed it once it had uploaded.

"You need anything? A drink or something?" Caite asked.

"Nah. I'm good. Getting tired, though. Think you can convince my compatriots over there that it's time to head home?"

She laughed ruefully, watching Nellie and Pax posing for picture after picture. Neither of them seemed tired. "Not sure about that. But you're done with this promo stuff in…five minutes. You can all do whatever you want."

He hadn't let go of her shoulders and now half turned toward her. "Yeah? Whatever I want?"

"Are you flirting with me?" she teased, getting ready to step out of the way so that a girl with white-blond ponytails could get him to sign her half-bared breasts.

"Only if you're interested," he said, holding up his pen with a flourish that made the blonde girl squeal.

Caite had to think on that for a second or so as she looked out over the jostling crowd. There were at least a hundred girls in here tonight who'd give their right arm for a wink and smile from Tommy Sanders, much less something a little more personal. Before she could answer, he backed up a step to put an arm around her again, this time to nuzzle against her ear.

"Only if the wolf over there wouldn't bite my head off," Tommy said.

Caite followed his gaze. "Jamison? He's my boss."

"He's looking at you like he wants to gobble you up. Hey there, what's your name?" And that was it—Tommy was back to being famous, signing boobs and posing for pictures in the last five minutes before their gig ended.

And Caite had managed to get them trending in the top five social media sites, at least for half an hour.

"Not bad," Jamison said. "Are they ready to leave yet?"

"Tommy is. Nellie and Paxton aren't. Let me guess. You are." Caite waved for a glass of ice water. The press of the crowd had left her sweating. Or maybe it had been the hint from Tommy that her boss might be interested in her. That was good for a spike in her heart rate.

"You think they're going to keep their shit together?"

Caite looked out to the dance floor, where Nellie was grinding with Pax, both of them bathed in the glare of a dozen flashes going off. Tommy joined them in a moment, bumping her ass while she shimmied. "Um…do we care?"

"We're being paid to care."

She gave their clients another long look, then looked back at Jamison. "They're off the clock as of ten minutes ago. Whatever they do now is on their own time. Nellie can't go more than five minutes without posting selfies of herself. Pax, too. Tommy has a handle on what's good promo. They've been doing this for two seasons. Unless you think something's going to burn down tonight, I'd say we can leave them to their drinking and debauchery and head home."

Jamison gave her a long look. "You don't want to stay? Dance? Drink? Maybe get a little snuggly with Tommy over there?"

So. He had noticed them talking. Interesting.

Caite grinned. "He's too busy with his legions of screaming fans for the likes of li'l ole me. Anyway, I just want to get
home and take off these shoes and get into bed."

For a moment, she thought he might say something more,
but Jamison only nodded. "Share a cab?"

"Sure thing, Boss."

"You don't have to call me that," he said when they slid into
the backseat of the taxi and he'd given the driver her address.

"No?" Caite stifled a yawn with the back of her hand, glad
to be out of the club's pounding beat and flashing lights. She'd
done her share of clubbing in her time and still enjoyed a night
out dancing. But that place had been over-the-top crowded
and too trendy for her tastes. "I thought maybe you'd like it."

"Well. I don't."

"Huh." She eyed him. "You know, in all the time I've
worked for you, I don't think we've done more than share a
couple words here and there."

He'd been looking out the window at the passing streets
but turned toward her now. "And?"

"Well. That's a little strange, don't you think? At the very
least, bordering on unfriendly." She was teasing him a little,
though there was an undercurrent of truth in her words.

"You think I'm unfriendly?" He frowned. "Since when
does working with someone require you to be best friends?"

"You're best friends with Elise," she pointed out, more curious about his reaction than because she harbored any sort of
long-term resentments. Up until just now, the fact that one of
her two bosses pretty much left her alone had been a bonus,
not a complaint.

"I've known her since high school." He looked out the window again. "You actually live in this neighborhood?"

The cab slowed to a stop in front of her building. Caite
leaned forward to offer the driver her credit card, but Jamison's

hand closed over her wrist and tugged it away. She glanced at him. "Yes. I do. Hey, I've got this."

"You don't." His big hand nearly engulfed hers, and his expression brooked no argument.

"I'd have billed it to the company," she said with a small grin.

Jamison didn't smile as he paid the driver. He looked again outside. "I'm walking you to your door."

Two feelings battled inside her at his words. First the taken-aback and slightly insulted feeling of him judging her neighborhood, which, admittedly, wasn't the greatest. Especially at almost two in the morning. The second, though, was ooey gooey and spreading warm electric tingles that started somewhere in the vicinity of her belly and quickly moved definitely lower.

"You don't have to do that, Jamison. I'll be fine," Caite said, but Jamison waved her to silence.

"I'm making sure you get inside. No arguing." He slid along the bench seat behind her, both of them getting out onto the cracked cobblestone pavement just down from her building. She thought she heard him mutter something about how being unfriendly didn't mean he wasn't also a gentleman.

"I never said you weren't a gentleman," Caite told him as she struggled to open her front door. The lock stuck. There was a trick to getting the key to slide in just right....

Which Jamison, apparently, had mastered, because he took the key from her hand and pushed it into the lock, then twisted, getting the door to open. It creaked, skidding along the tile floor of the entryway as it always did because it hung unevenly on the hinges. He cringed.

"It's an old building," Caite said, hating that she felt as though she had to apologize for the wear and tear. "I like it. It's got charm."

Without asking, he followed her up the creaking, slanted stairs and into her living room. She hadn't left a light burning when she left this morning, but the pale glow coming in through the windows was enough for her to get to the switch on the wall. With the room bathed in golden light from the dark-shaded lamps, it didn't look too bad, and she gave herself a mental kick for even daring for a second to feel as though her home were something to be ashamed of. She liked her old building with its charms and quirks.

"It looks like you," he said.

Caite thought about that for a moment, looking around to see it the way he did. "Thanks. But you really don't know me. Do you?"

"You've established that." He looked…embarrassed?

"You want something to drink?" Caite gave him a curious glance as she slung her purse onto the hooks she'd attached to the wall next to the front door and moved toward the narrow hallway leading back to the kitchen. "How about some food? I'm starving."

"I should get going," he said from behind her, but followed.

He looked too big for her tiny kitchen. Whoever had designed this apartment had been generous in carving out the living room and bedrooms from what had formerly been a single home, but the kitchen and bathroom had been given short shrift. Jamison loomed over the wee oven, the three-quarters-size fridge, the small porcelain sink. There wasn't room in there for a table, just a couple stools pushed against the bar built into the half wall separating the kitchen from the dining room. He didn't have to hunch his shoulders to keep his head from hitting the ceiling or anything, but with those broad shoulders and long legs, he definitely filled up a lot of the space.

"I can make scrambled eggs and toast," Caite said, the words skidding around her suddenly dry throat. "Nothing's better than breakfast when you come home from the club."

He shook his head but made no move to leave. Caite poked one of the stools toward him. He sat.

She didn't understand him. Not one bit. But instead of finding that annoying or intimidating, all it did was make her want to know him better.

The food was ready in minutes, simple eggs and sourdough toast with real butter and jam on two pretty, delicate china plates she'd picked up at some holiday sale last year. She had orange juice, too. Coffee would've been good, but she did intend to sleep, and soon.

"Oh," she said as she slid the plates onto the bar. "And this!"

A plate of homemade scones from the authentic British bakery down the street, complete with thick, rich clotted cream. She put the plate between them and took a seat on the stool, handing Jamison a fork as she did. He took it but absently, his attention on the phone in his hand.

"Hey. Enough. You can check the stats and stuff in the morning. Eat, now." That it already was the morning didn't escape her, but she wasn't going to point that out.

"Nellie's drunk-tweeting." Jamison's mouth twisted in distaste.

"Um, that's what she does." Caite snagged his phone from his hand. "Ah, ah, ah. Be a good boy and eat your food before it's cold."

For a moment, heat blazed in his eyes, and she thought he was going to lose his temper. She held his phone just out of reach, gauging if he'd grab for it. Wondering what she would do if he did.

Something grew between them.

Something thick with anticipation. Her heart thudded faster. In her fist the phone had become heavy as a brick. Her nipples had gone tight and hard as she stared him down. Her breath caught, watching him give in to her.

Without another word, Jamison turned to his food and picked up the fork. He stabbed a bite of eggs and chewed them slowly. Silent. Caite set the phone between them on the bar, where he could easily reach it if he wanted to, and again Caite wondered if he'd take it. She would've, if it had been hers. But Jamison only ate, using the thickly buttered toast to push the eggs onto his fork.

"It's good," he said in a low voice. "Thanks. I was really hungry."

"I know you were. You didn't eat much at dinner, and if you don't eat every few hours, you get really cranky."

He paused with the fork halfway to his mouth, then set it down. "How...?"

"Look, just because you've barely given me a glance for months doesn't mean I don't pay attention to what goes on in the office." Caite nibbled her toast for a second, then washed it down with sweet orange juice. "The yelling starts right around eleven-thirty and tapers off after lunch until about three. Here. You need to have some of this—it's excellent."

She held up a scone and dripped the clotted cream all over it. But when she tried to hand it to him, Jamison shook his head. Caite waved it closer, tempting, but he wouldn't be tempted.

"I don't eat that sort of thing."

"You should," she told him, not putting it down. "Every once in a while, you need a little something sweet. Everyone does."

There it was again. That rising heat. That anticipation, the tension between them. Caite looked into Jamison's eyes and didn't let her gaze waver, didn't put down the scone. She waited.

"No, thanks."

She put the scone on the plate and licked a few drops of cream from her fingertips, watching the way his eyes followed the motion of her tongue. Her stomach tumbled. He was her boss. This was dangerous territory. But there was no denying that something was going on here. She glanced at the phone he hadn't reached for. More heat filled her, this time centering between her thighs.

Stupid, she told herself as she leaned over the bar to tug a silk scarf from a tangle of similar accessories she'd left on the dining room sideboard. This was stupid and dangerous, and she could lose her job....She held the scarf aloft.

"You need to learn to let go sometimes, Jamison."

He eyed her warily. "You seem to think so."

It was the perfect time for him to get up and leave. Closing in on 3:00 a.m., stomach full, no reason for him to stay. But he didn't move.

Caite drew the silk between her fingers, enjoying the smooth fabric on her skin. "Close your eyes."

# 4

CAITE WAITED FOR him to scoff. Or sneer. But he didn't. Jamison closed his eyes, and was that the slightest tremble of his lips she saw? The tiniest hitch of his breath?

Her hands shook a little when she tied the scarf around his eyes and smoothed it onto his cheeks. It was an imperfect blindfold; if he tried hard enough, surely he'd be able to see. But Jamison didn't move. Standing between his legs, Caite didn't move, either.

"Open your mouth," she breathed, certain this time he'd have to deny her. He'd have to.

But he didn't. Jamison's lips parted, the hint of his tongue making her want to lean in close and taste him. She didn't, of course. Kiss her boss? Craziness, even if, dear God, he smelled so good this close that it made her knees a little weak.

Caite took a fingerful of cream from on top of the scones and let it touch the center of his lower lip. "Taste it."

His tongue crept out. A shiver ran through her. His breath sighed out. She traced his lower lip again with the cream, this time adding a little more.

"Again."

This time his breath shuddered out of him, and Caite put a hand on his shoulder to keep herself from having to sit. They stayed very close, neither moving. Below the blindfold, Jamison's mouth looked even more lush and inviting.

"When you can't see," she said in a low voice, "it's so much easier to give up. Isn't it?"

His hands skimmed up the sides of her thighs to settle on her hips. She didn't imagine the way his head tilted or his fingers tightened, pulling her a little closer. The heat that had been simmering between them became white-hot.

Fuck this—she was going to kiss him.

His phone bleated, then buzzed against the wooden breakfast bar. Jamison's grip loosened. He pushed back from her a little, tugging at the blindfold to grab his phone. He didn't look at her as he thumbed the screen and typed in his password.

He looked at the text message, then at her. The cream had vanished from his mouth, which was good since nothing about his expression looked anything close to sweet. "Your girl Nellie just got herself arrested."

It was actually a bonus, as far as these things went. For the company. A chance to prove that Wolfe and Baron could put a positive spin on negative situations meant that something bad had to happen first. So it wasn't that Jamison was pissed that Caite's new clients had gotten themselves into trouble.

It wasn't that at all.

No, it was the memory of the way her fingertip had drifted over his lower lip. The taste of her mingled with the sweet clotted cream. It was knowing, deep in his gut, that her mouth would be as delicious. Her pussy even sweeter. It was thinking about how sleek the silk had been against his face, the darkness against his closed eyes. The press of his rock-hard cock inside his trousers.

All of that had put him in the worst of moods, along with the lack of sleep and having to work on a Saturday. When the call came in, Caite had calmly begun handling it in a way that had impressed him, though he wasn't willing to tell her so. Not yet. He'd been expecting to take over a bulk of work when Elise had the baby, but now with her on extended leave, having Caite take over her clients would relieve him of a lot of work and stress…and perversely, he wasn't willing to let that all go. He'd worked too hard to build Wolfe and Baron not to cling to it. Not even if Caite Fox had her head on straight and seemed to know what she was doing. With everything.

Again his cock throbbed as he thought of how she'd taken his phone. The way she'd known so much about him already, anticipating what he'd need or want. The simple act of making him food when he hadn't had to tell her he was hungry. Her quiet commands. Jamison closed his eyes, swallowing hard against the remembered touch of her fingertips to his lips.

"Open your mouth," she'd said, and he had, immediately. Without hesitation, responding to her steady confidence. The impression that she expected him to do as she said without question had been like putting a match to gasoline for him. She'd said it as if she owned him, and he'd let her.

That was the worst part.

"Shit," he muttered, scrubbing at his eyes. Not enough sleep and not enough coffee.

From the couch across from him, Caite stirred, and Jamison quieted. Watching her. They'd spent the past few hours putting the spin on the Nellie situation. They hadn't had to post her bail or pick her up—her management team did that. But he and Caite had done their share of Connexing, tweeting and posting links to positive updates about the incident, along with putting out official statements. Would it work? Time would tell, but instead of a flood of angry social media chatter about the fact Nellie had punched a girl in the face, they'd managed to at least twist the story to suggest it had been in self-defense. The other girl had tossed a drink in her face, called her names. Something like that. Jamison was too tired to care.

"Morning," Caite said. She stretched like a cat, one limb at a time, and pushed her honey-blond hair back from her face. She leaned forward to rub her hands on her knees. "Time is it?"

"Just past eight."

"God. I wanted to sleep until at least nine today." She eyed him. "Did you sleep at all?"

"Some."

"In that chair?" She pointed.

Jamison nodded. Caite got up and crossed to him on bare feet. At some point during the night or early morning, as it were, she'd changed into soft pajama pants and a T-shirt. He'd declined her offer of a pair of sweats but had conceded to loosening his tie. Now she stood in front of him, and before he could stop her, she put a fingertip beneath his chin and tilted it upward.

"You didn't sleep." She leaned close to look into his eyes. "You're going to be a mess."

"I'll sleep when I go home."

"Are you going home?" She hadn't moved away. Hadn't taken her fingers from beneath his chin.

His throat closed. Heart began to thud harder. He blinked, unable to look away from her.

"Jamison," Caite said slowly. "We did a good job, huh? Got things back on track, right?"

"Yes. It seems so."

"You should go to sleep." Still, neither of them moved. She studied him. "You could've left. But you didn't."

"I wanted to make sure we got this under control."

"Because you don't trust me?" she asked.

He had to admit it was true. Caite didn't seem offended. She smiled faintly.

"Because you like to be in control," she whispered. "All the time."

"I…Yeah," he said, and it was the truth but felt like a lie.

"I told you, you should learn to let go a little."

This close, her eyes were wide and dark but not brown the way he'd thought. He caught glints of gold and green. She had the faintest lines in the corners, too. She spent a lot of time smiling, then.

"I don't like—" he began.

Her hand slid from under his chin to the back of his head, where her fingers gripped his hair, tipping his face up. She wasn't hurting him, but he let out a low groan he stifled at once. She didn't laugh or even smile. If she had, he'd have been out of there before she could say a word.

"Shhh," she whispered. "Shhh."

Jamison quieted. Every muscle had gone tense, but when Caite fitted herself onto his lap, tiny tremors began to ripple through him. She cupped his face in her hands. He could not look away.

"Don't you want," she said, "to give up a little control? Just a little?"

He hadn't wanted anything so much, ever, but dammit if that didn't piss him off even more. "Get off me."

But when she tried, his hands on her hips kept her still. They stared at each other. A breath in. A breath out. Never looking away from each other's eyes.

"You should get off," he whispered.

"Oh, I'd love to," Caite said. "I'd like to get off very much."

His cock surged at the innuendo. His fingers gripped her smooth, warm skin just above the waistband of her pajamas. The feeling of it made him want to get on his knees in front of her. To open her thighs and use his mouth on her. To hear her cry out his name as she came.

Jamison didn't move.

Caite rocked her hips the tiniest amount, pressing herself against the bulge in his pants. Her eyes never left his. "When's the last time you fucked a woman, not your hand?"

He said nothing.

"When," she said, rocking a little harder, "is the last time you came?"

It had been just over a week, but he kept his mouth closed tight. He could stand, tumbling her off his lap, but something stopped him. The look in her eyes? The sound of her voice. The way her hands felt on his face as she kept him still, forcing him to look into her eyes.

"I'm going to kiss you," Caite said softly but firmly. "Are you going to let me?"

Jamison meant to say "No," but what came out was nothing but a sigh. She tilted her head. Her lips brushed his, but she didn't kiss him. Not yet. She let her breath caress him, teasing. The weight of her on his lap was so slight it was like holding air, and yet the pressure of her body on his erection was enough to make him grunt in frustration when she rocked on him again.

His mouth opened, seeking hers, but she held him still.

"No," she said. "I told you, I'm going to kiss *you*."

He waited, heart pounding so hard he swore he could hear the thunder of it outside his chest. He counted the seconds, the breaths, the pulse of blood in his engorged prick. He thought he would tell her to get the fuck off his lap. He thought he'd turn his head to keep his mouth from hers, but in the end all he did was wait for Caite to kiss him.

She did.

And he was lost.

★ ★ ★

Caite slanted her mouth to Jamison's, the press of her lips light at first but quickly getting harder as soon as he opened for her. The soft sigh of his moan against her lips sent a shiver through her, but what really got her going was the way he totally succumbed to her. She'd noticed it a few times already, his reactions to the way she took command. Every time she'd thought he would balk or outright refuse her, he had not, and he wasn't now. It set her on fire.

"You work hard," she told him now, every word brushing her mouth on his. "But you have to learn to let a few things go."

His fingers tightened on her hips, digging just hard enough to promise pain if he kept going. He didn't. Caite wasn't sure if she was relieved or disappointed.

"If you want something done right, you have to make sure you do it yourself," Jamison breathed.

"Okay. Boss."

"I told you not to call me that."

Caite laughed, then paused, waiting for the subtle feeling of his body straining toward hers. When she felt it, that tension, the flex and release of his muscles and the soft caress of his breath on her mouth, she brushed his lips with hers again. She wanted to take his mouth and plunder it, fuck into it with her tongue while she pulled his hair so tight he couldn't move… except he could move—that was the thrill of it. He could toss her off his lap. Push her away. She couldn't control him, not physically, unless he let her, and oh, shit, he was letting her.

"You don't hover over Elise."

Jamison licked his lips, touching hers with his tongue. "You're not Elise."

She'd have been pissed off if she weren't so turned on. She

held his face a little tighter, tipping it up. "Thank God for that, or else you wouldn't be rock hard right now."

He did try to pull away then, but not with enough force to make her let him go. Caite ground herself against him a little harder. She meant it to tease him, but it felt so good that she shuddered. It had been months since her last relationship ended, and she hadn't had so much as a one-nighter since then. Touching him, tasting him, all she could think about was feeling him inside her.

"You taste so good," she whispered into his mouth. "Open. Let me taste you more."

Surely this time he'd refuse her. Put her off his lap, stalk out the door. Hell, maybe he'd fire her for good measure. But no, Jamison's mouth opened and he gave her his tongue. His cock, thick and hard and, oh, shit, yes, throbbing, pushed against her clit. She wore only a thin pair of flannel pj bottoms and no panties, and every movement rubbed her bare pussy against the soft fabric.

"That feels so good," she murmured, rocking her hips.

His hands tightened again. He kissed her harder, and she let him. Their teeth clashed. Tongues battled. His hands slid down to cup her ass, pushing her against him harder. Faster. Together they rocked so hard the chair creaked.

Her orgasm coiled tight and tighter, building. She was going to come from this—not from just the consistent, delicious pressure of her clit against him but from everything else. The way he'd given in to her. The way he shuddered now.

"Oh," she said, surprised. "Yes. Right there. Like that."

Pleasure filled her like a river rushing through a canyon. She shook with it, her hands still cupping his face. Her mouth on his. The copper taste of blood forced her eyes open—she'd nipped his lower lip. Jamison didn't seem to care, his own eyes closed, cock still hard and pushing against her. When she quieted, sighing his name, he opened his eyes.

Something nameless twisted between them.

Caite swallowed, licking her lips of the last taste of him. She drew in a breath, blinking to clear her head. With someone else she'd be reaching between them to unzip him, to get her hands on him. Maybe her mouth. But...

"No," she said in a low voice. Then, louder, as she got off his lap, "No, I don't think so. I think you should go now."

# 5

"HOLD MY CALLS," Jamison said to Bobby without so much as a "Good morning" to warm him up. Bobby didn't look surprised, at least not until Jamison added, "and hold all of Ms. Fox's calls, too."

"But...she's—" Bobby began.

Jamison silenced him with a stare. He didn't give a good goddamn what Caite was doing. In about ten minutes she was going to be doing whatever he wanted her to do.

He'd left her apartment when she told him to, his prick so hard it ached. It had stayed that way on and off for most of the weekend. He'd edged himself in the shower and at bedtime, then again when he woke up on Sunday, teasing himself almost to completion over and over until he'd had only to lie back and remember Caite's mouth on his in order to come without even touching himself. The climax had been fierce enough to leave him blinded for a few seconds, faint stars swirling in his vision.

It hadn't helped.

He'd woken this morning with another raging hard-on and the lingering taste of her teasing him. He'd spent the morning drive thinking of all the ways he was going to deal with what had happened, everything ranging from simply firing her to bending her over his desk and taking her from behind. Now, striding down the hall toward her office, he thought he'd fist his hands in her hair and make her get on her knees. Shit, he thought as he pushed open her door without even knocking, he should give her a severance and be done.

"Yes, I saw it. Yep. Okay. Sure, no problem," Caite was saying as she turned to stare at him when he burst through her door and shut it behind him. Her eyebrows rose, but she ended the call quickly and before he could say a word, she said, "How rude."

His mouth had opened to let out all the words he'd imagined, but at that simple truth from her, Jamison shut up immediately. He'd never met a woman who could do that to him with little more than an arch of her brow. He clenched his fists.

"Sit down," Caite said calmly, pointing to the chair in front of her desk.

He did.

She came around the front to sit on the desk's edge, and, oh, fuck him, her plain dark skirt rode up just enough to show off the lacy edge of a pair of thigh-high stockings. How had he never noticed her in all these months? Jamison glowered.

"You look like you have something to say to me, Jamison."

"Oh, I have a lot to say to you."

Caite laughed, damn her. Laughed and shook her head as though he were a naughty schoolboy brought into the principal's office for pulling a girl's pigtails. Her dark eyes twinkled when she looked back at him.

"You're angry with me?"

He…was. And wasn't. If anything, he was furious with himself for allowing her to do what she'd done. "I'm your boss."

"I thought you said you didn't want me to call you that," she teased.

He drew in a breath, then another to calm himself. "I'm not in the habit of fucking around with my employees."

"I see." Caite crossed her arms and tilted her head to study him.

He waited for her to say something else, but she didn't. "We can't do that again."

"I see," she repeated, and shifted a little on the desk, revealing a bit more bare thigh he did his best to ignore. "Let me ask you something. Why are you so angry about it?"

He took in another breath but had no words. Being left speechless made him angry. So did the calm way she stared him down. But ultimately, he couldn't articulate an answer.

"I think I know," she said quietly. "It's because you're a man who's always in charge. Right? Always in control. You're used to getting what you want when you want it and how. And you don't really trust someone else to get it right."

"If you want to make sure something's done right, you have to do it yourself."

"You like to take care of people."

He had to think about that. His anger had faded in the face of her continued calm. She was like Elise in that way, a foil to his easily ignited fury. "I don't know what you mean."

"You made sure I got home safe. You didn't have to."

"Of course I did. You're mine.... You're my employee. It would've been irresponsible of me to just dump you off in that neighborhood at that time of night." He didn't miss the way his stumbled words had made her smile.

Caite studied him a little longer. "Let me ask you a question, Jamison. Don't you ever get...tired?"

He did. Oh, God, did he ever. Not of things in the office, not of being on top of things there. He thrived on that stuff.

But in the rest of his life…the never-ending parade of dinner reservations that didn't please women who didn't like to eat, the flowers for others who'd rather have chocolate. The concerts of bands he loved and they'd never heard of and hated.

"Yes," he said. "I do."

Caite resettled herself on the edge of the desk, uncrossing her legs. Her fingers curled into the hem of her skirt, inching it higher while Jamison could only sit there like an idiot, watching. "I dreamed about you. What we did. Kissing you. I dreamed about your kiss, Jamison."

His mouth went dry. His cock, hard. His heart pounded.

Higher, higher, she eased the fabric over her thighs, exposing the sexy-as-hell gartered stockings he'd already glimpsed. He'd never been with a woman who wore stockings like that outside the bedroom and not as part of a costume. He wanted to look away from the promise being revealed between her legs and had to force himself to meet her eyes.

"You're going to get on your knees for me," Caite whispered. "You're going to put your mouth on me, right here. And make me come with that delicious mouth of yours. Now."

Everything about it screamed wrong. The office setting, her place in the company. The fact that she was the one telling him what to do. And still, Jamison slid from his chair to kneel in front of her, his hands already skimming up the backs of her legs, his mouth already seeking her heat. No thought. No resistance.

Only desire.

She shuddered when he mouthed the softness of her inner thigh just above the stocking. The soft growl of her moan sent another bolt of desire straight through him, tightening his balls and making his dick throb in time to his quickening pulse. When her hand came to rest on top of his head, fingers tangling in his hair, he nipped at her flesh a little harder than he'd intended.

"Fuck, yes," Caite cried, jerking. "Oh. God."

She wore filmy white panties and he hooked a finger in them to pull them aside to get at her pussy. His head spun at the scent of her, but when he got his mouth on her hot flesh, everything else faded away. There was nothing but this. Her heat, the slickness of her pussy on his lips and then fingers when he pushed them inside her. The tight knot of her clit tempted him to suckle gently and, then she cried out again, hips bucking, a little harder.

This was crazy stupid, and not only because they were at work. Because she worked for him, under him...beneath... Shit, he was nowhere near on top of things right now. And he had no idea how he'd ended up here or why it was making him so insane.

From down the hall came the sound of ringing phones. The murmur of voices. Shit, he thought, moving away from her. The office door. Not locked. And Bobby...

"The door," Jamison said against her.

Caite's fingers tightened in his hair, keeping him close to her. He could pull away if he wanted to. He didn't want to.

"Keep going."

He paused despite the command, picturing Bobby opening the door and catching his boss going down on the junior assistant. Caite laughed, the full, throaty and rich sound of it making him even harder, if that were possible. Her hand came down to cup his chin, fingers pinching slightly.

"Keep going," Caite said, her gaze bright. Cheeks flushed. Her mouth was wet, as if she'd licked it. "I didn't say you could stop."

He'd brought her to orgasm once already by barely doing a thing. He could make her come again, this time with his tongue, in another few minutes. If he wanted to. If he did as she said. If he obeyed.

From behind him, the doorknob rattled. Caite let go of his face. He could've moved away but did not.

"Make me come, Jamison," Caite whispered, her gaze going over his shoulder as both of them waited for the door to open. It didn't. She looked down at him. "Now."

He feasted on her, a starving man who hadn't even known he was hungry. She rocked against him. Her clit, tight and hard under his lips and tongue, tempted him to suck it again. He slid a finger inside her. Then another. Stroking upward, slow and easy, not too hard. He wanted to touch himself but did not, masochistically satisfied with the pressure of his cock against the front of his pants making him even crazier.

When her pussy tightened around his fingers, she cried out, low and hoarse. Then again. His name. A framed picture on her desk fell over, and her thighs clamped hard against his head, blocking out the light for a moment. Blocking out sound. All he could see or hear, all he could smell and taste, was Caite's sweet cunt, and in that moment, he'd have happily died with her flavor the last thing he ever tasted.

She leaned back on the desk, her knees falling open to release him. He sat back on his heels. Caite looked down at him, her eyes glazed and face flushed. She swallowed hard and swept her lips with her tongue. Then she took a deep sighing breath.

"Wow," she said.

She shook herself a little, then sat up straight, pulling down her skirt. She passed a hand over her hair, which had become only a tiny bit disheveled. She smiled at him, saying nothing, and he was glad for it, because that meant he didn't have to answer. He got to his feet, his cock thick with arousal, his balls heavy and aching. He adjusted himself, but it gave little relief. He wanted to be inside her. Or have her mouth on him, her hands. He'd spill himself between her breasts if she let him. All he could think about, really, was getting off....

Her doorknob rattled again, and this time she looked over his shoulder. "Come in. Hi, Bobby."

"There's a delivery for you. Flowers," Bobby said. "They came from Tommy."

Caite looked surprised. "Okay. Thanks."

When Bobby left the office, she looked at Jamison, still saying nothing. He cleared his throat and unfisted his hands, unaware that he'd been clenching them until she gave them a pointed stare. His fingers ached. He kept himself from holding his hand to his face to breathe her in.

"Was there something else you needed? Boss?"

Dammit, she was teasing him again, though her expression was completely innocent and her tone neutral. Jamison shook his head, backing up a step. If she let her gaze fall to the front of his pants, he thought, he would lock her office door and spin her around, hands on the desk....She kept her eyes on his, that faint smile never twisting or fading.

"No," Jamison said. "Nothing."

Caite had visited a movie set once, back in college when she'd hung out with all the artsy types who wanted to be directors. Her boyfriend's boyfriend—it had been complicated, yeah—had been hired as an intern on a movie shooting in New York City over the summer, and Caite and Leo had been invited up for the day. It had been hot, the city had smelled like urine, and she'd ended up with food poisoning from the craft services table. The movie had gone straight to rental, and she'd never even seen it.

*Treasure House* was an entirely different matter. Tommy had invited her to come to the site after work on Friday to live-tweet during their final filming of the week, a series of teasers that would air to promote the next week's show.

"It's for what we filmed two weeks ago but will air next week," he explained. "But the network wants us to start getting the word out now. Teasing. You know."

She did. And that was what she was being paid for, to decide what and how and where to put out the message about this show and its three stars. While the three got set up, each filming an individual teaser for several different markets, then group teasers, Caite set up and sent out short video clips and updates to all the social media outlets she could. It wasn't exhausting work by any means, but even so it *was* long past five o'clock on a Friday night. And even fun work was still work.

"You coming out with us tonight?" Nellie used a makeup-remover cloth to swipe at the thick foundation she'd worn for the filming. She eyed Caite. "Tommy says he refuses to go clubbing. Says he wants to have dinner in a nice place with tablecloths and then…God, go to some art exhibit. I said we could go clubbing after, but he's telling us we got to pick last weekend. Maybe you can change his mind."

Caite looked up from her phone, where she'd been typing in a final update to a fan page. "What makes you think I could do that?"

"He likes you." Nellie simpered. Not a good look for her. "I bet if you said you'd go clubbing, he'd come so he could spend time with you."

Faintly surprised, but only faintly, Caite looked across the room to where Tommy was tucking some things into a messenger bag. He looked good. Faded jeans that hit him in all the right places. Black T-shirt that hugged his slim body and revealed strong arms patterned with colorful tattoos. He was not only her type as if he'd seen a checklist of what she liked and made himself over to fit it, but he was also surprisingly charming, something she'd never have guessed from watching the show, where he was most often the angry one, yelling at the others to get their shit together.

Shit, she thought, thinking of Jamison. She really did have a type.

Still, what had happened with her boss had been a delicious but definite mistake. He'd barely spoken to her since it had happened and had been keeping his office door closed. There'd been hours of work and little of it completed by the end of the week, even though she'd thrown herself into all of it in order to forget. She got the hint and was sort of glad, too, that he was avoiding her rather than making all of it into something bigger than it had to be. Except…wasn't it? Bigger than it should've been, Caite thought, watching Tommy head toward her with a broad smile on his face. Because she hadn't been able to stop thinking about Jamison's mouth and hands, the look on his face. The sound of his moans.

She was so fucked.

Jamison had blown into her office and then gone down on her as if cunnilingus were about to be outlawed and he needed to stock up so he could supply the black market. Yes, she'd basically ordered him to, and yes, she'd made it out as though she were totally in charge, but the truth was, every part of what had happened had shaken her to the core. After he'd made her come with his mouth, her climax so explosive she swore she'd almost lost consciousness for half a minute, he'd gotten to his feet and stared down at her as though waiting for her to say something. Do something. And she'd messed it up, hadn't she? Uncertain of what to say, her knees still weak and her mind awhirl with the fact he'd even done it. Again. That he'd given himself up to her. Again. And without getting him off, no reciprocity, nothing for him but a rock-hard dick and probably a set of blue balls. He'd left her office without a word, shutting the door firmly behind him.

But fucking around with her boss was one thing. Doing it with a client could only lead to worse trouble. Jamison could fire her for what they'd done, but if she screwed this up, it would not only affect her job with Wolfe and Baron but any job she had in the future. If there was one thing she'd learned fast about working in the media business, it was that fucking celebrities never led to the kind of reputation that did anyone any good.

"Hi," she said, pushing thoughts of her hot-as-hell boss and her future career to the side for a moment. "What's up?"

"Want to come out with us? Dinner at L'Etoile. My treat. Then I'm dragging those yahoos over to the Scott Church gallery show."

"And after that?" she asked, curious. Nellie had gone over to linger with Pax, the two of them doing that annoying whispering thing again.

Tommy looked at his partners. "They want to go clubbing. But shit, I'm tired. Long week, lots of shit went down...."

"Like what?"

He laughed and wagged a finger. "Ah, ah, ah. Can't tell you. You have to tune in."

"Is that where you got the shiner?" Caite touched his cheekbone gently.

Tommy leaned a little closer. "Maybe I got that from my domina."

Caite blinked. Blinked again. She had no idea what to say to that; all she knew was that the idea of Tommy having a domina made her tingle in all the right places. Maybe for the wrong reasons, though.

"Relax, cupcake. It's from running into a door in the dark. At least, that's what I need to tweet, right?" Tommy grinned.

Caite laughed. He took her hand, squeezing lightly. "Come with us. It'll be fun."

"What the hell," Caite said. "Sure. Why not?"

# 6

"WHAT THE HELL were you thinking?" Jamison tossed a sheaf of printed pages onto the conference room table. Bobby'd printed out all the latest media updates. They scattered, but he didn't bother to pick them up.

Caite didn't, either. She sat with her hands folded neatly on the tabletop. Today she wore a crisp white shirt and a black skirt. Black pumps. Her honey-blond hair had been pulled into a neat French twist, and in her ears were creamy pearl studs. Her bare throat, uncollared by any jewelry, taunted him.

So did her mouth.

"I'm not sure what you're getting at," she said.

"All of these pictures. The video." Jamison tilted the conference room's laptop toward her to show off the screen, which showed a picture of Caite and that asshole Tommy whatever-the-fuck-his-name-was doing shots. And dancing. And laughing. Not kissing, but there was the suggestion of that, too. And lots of commentary about it.

"*Treasure House* Tommy's new gal pal," he said, reading one of the comments.

Caite snorted. "Oh, brother."

Jamison was as far from laughing as the sun from Pluto. "This isn't what we pay you for."

Caite's laughter cut off abruptly. She sat up higher in her chair, shoulders squaring. One eyebrow lifted, but her fingers didn't even twitch. "What's that supposed to mean?"

"It means that your job's to keep these forons in the public view in a positive light, not…not…" He stopped himself before his voice could rise into a shout, though he wanted it to.

"Not…have fun? Not mix business with pleasure? Not get the buzz going about them? You are aware that last night's Buzzvid clip was rebuzzed more than a thousand times, and that the Wolfe and Baron account got more than five hundred new followers? I don't know how many each of the three *Treasure House* accounts got, but the comments were in the thousands, too." Her chin went up a little bit. "Compared to the night Nellie got arrested, I'm pretty sure we got a lot more positive growth from a few pictures of us all having a good time."

He didn't want to think about the night Nellie had been arrested. Or what had happened afterward, in Caite's apartment. Or why what had happened was making him so angry now.

"You're not supposed to be having a good time with…him."

Now both her eyebrows lifted, and her lips parted on a huff of surprise. "I wasn't aware that anything I choose to do when I'm not on the clock is any of your business."

"It is when it reflects on the reputation of this company." Jamison heard the words spitting from his mouth. He even believed them. But at the same time, he knew he was full of shit.

Caite pushed her chair away from the table and stood. Aside from the slight tremble in her voice when she answered him, she was perfectly calm. "If you don't like the way I do my job, Mr. Wolfe, then I suggest you find a replacement."

Silence swelled between them, sharp as glass, as knives. Hot as a dying star. They stared each other down, neither of them moving. Scarcely a blink. Barely a breath.

At last, Caite smoothed the front of her skirt and tucked a nonexistent strand of hair behind her ear. "Is that everything? Are you finished?"

"Dammit, Caite, just…listen to me."

She stabbed at the air between them. "No. You listen. I've worked my ass off for this company for eight months, most of those completely under your radar. I've done everything you and Elise asked of me plus more. You might not like it, but I started taking on a lot more responsibility even before she got sick. So while you might think you've done me some huge favor by letting me take on these clients, the truth is, it's the other way around. You want to talk to me about the reputation of this company? Really? Why? Because you're jealous?"

He *was* jealous. That was the truth of it. He'd been unable to get the taste of her off his tongue for days, and the thought of another man kissing her…touching her…

"Do you think just because we fucked around," Caite said in a low voice, "that you…what? Own me?"

No. That wasn't it at all. Jamison owned an expensive watch, a nice car, furniture. A cell phone. He could never own her. Not that he wanted to, he told himself. And he sure as hell didn't want her to own him.

"What happened between us was unprofessional at best. Stupid at worst," he said. "And has nothing to do with anything else."

Her chin went up. Her eyes flinty. "I agree."

Dammit, that wasn't what he'd wanted her to say. The problem was, Jamison had no idea what he did want her to say. Or do. She'd had him turned upside down from the moment she'd taken control of him, and he hadn't been normal since.

"Like it or not, Ms. Fox, there's a reason why the name of

this company is Wolfe and Baron, and it's because I'm the one in charge here. Me. Not you. So you should know your place."

She hesitated, as though she meant to say something else, then let out a low, soft sound. Her expression softened, a shift in her gaze. A tiny quirk of her mouth that wasn't a smile but at least was better than a frown or the cold, grim line of her anger.

"Nothing happened with us," Caite murmured so softly he almost didn't hear it.

In a way he wished he hadn't, because hearing it meant that somehow she knew it mattered to him. "Just keep your personal life personal, Ms. Fox. Not on company time."

For another few seconds, he thought she meant to say more, but whatever words had filtered to her tongue she bit back. He hated the cold flatness in her look, as though they barely knew each other. Well...that was the truth, wasn't it? They barely did.

So why, then, he thought as he watched her leave the room without so much as a glance behind her, did he feel as if Caite Fox knew him better than anyone ever had?

*Independent.*

*Mouthy.*

*You're an aggressive, intimidating bitch.*

The words of not just one but a few of her boyfriends echoed in her memory as Caite at last gave up the pretense of trying to work and shut down her computer. Her phone had been blessedly silent for the past few hours, the updates she'd scheduled getting a sufficient number of shares and comments, but nothing she had to handle. She could give in, call it a day. Go home.

Nothing waited for her there but a bottle of wine she'd have to drink by herself—never a great idea. And darkness.

And quiet. Even the idea of a bubble bath with candles and a good book didn't really appeal to her. She didn't want to go home. Not alone, anyway.

For the first time in years, really, Caite was tired of being alone. Her longest relationship had lasted four years and ended amicably enough a couple years ago when she and Dallas had both agreed that his promotion and consequent transfer to California was as good a time as any for them to either make a permanent commitment or to call it quits. Ending it as friends had seemed the better deal. Since then, she'd dated. Not consistently but a lot. A few, not many, had become "boyfriends." But most of them had been nothing except a way to pass the time until she'd grown tired of the parade of first dates that had never been good enough to turn into second ones. Getting off the dating carousel had been a relief, and being alone had been a choice.

Now, though, all she could think about was…well, not the sex. Though it had been amazing. Fantastic. Mind-blowing. But not the sex. The connection.

She and Jamison had not fucked like strangers getting naked together for the first time. Hell. They hadn't even fucked, technically. He'd give her pleasure—twice! And left without it being reciprocated. And yet those two times with him had been more erotic, more fulfilling and more meaningful than a double fistful of simultaneous orgasms and the afterglow of pillow talk. They had started from different places and ended the same way, yet during it, had met in the middle and found each other as though they'd clasped hands in a dark room and shown each other the way to the light.

"Oh, ugh. Gross," Caite murmured. "Stupid. Fairy tales and firesides, this is not."

But…what harm could it do to fantasize about it? All the months she'd worked here, her boss had certainly tantalized her daydreams. The reality of him had been even better. So what if it wasn't going to happen again, it wasn't meant to last, it had been shifting, scattering castles of dust. So what if he'd made it beyond clear that kneeling in front of her had been… wrong. Unprofessional, he'd said. And stupid.

Stupid, all right. Stupid to think a man like Jamison Wolfe would ever be able to give her what she wanted and needed. Still. That didn't mean she couldn't remember that just for those brief moments, it had happened.

He had kneeled for her.

*And he'd loved it.*

With a groan, Caite settled back in her chair and closed her eyes to try and chase away the memory of his mouth on her. His glazed look when he'd stared up at her from between her legs. When he'd turned and left without so much as a hand job, all at her command. She couldn't stop herself from touching the pulse beating in the base of her throat. Then her wrists, where she pressed against the throbbing flow of her blood, which had gone heated and swift in her veins at the thought of his kiss.

It could never work. Boss, employee—they were worlds apart even without that impropriety. But Jamison had given her a taste of what Caite had always craved and had been unable to articulate or even admit to herself until he had responded to her commands. And now, having tasted it, the idea of never having it again was enough to make her want to throw something on the floor and break it.

She'd finished her work hours ago but had not gone home, and why? Hoping to catch a glimpse of Jamison, who'd been so clearly avoiding her. That more than anything had convinced her of his disgust. Jamison Wolfe was not a man to avoid anyone, ever, yet he'd almost made a career of pretending she didn't exist.

Now the office was quiet. Bobby gone. Jamison might have left, too, but she didn't think so. With a shivering sigh, the residual memory of his mouth on her cunt making her breath catch, Caite put both her hands flat on the desk. Thinking about every cruel thing any man had ever said to her.

*You should know your place.*

That last had hurt worse than anything else. Her place? What was her place, exactly? Below, beneath, less than? And why? Because she was a woman?

"Fuck that," she said aloud, though the harsh words didn't chase away the taste of bitterness.

It had been two weeks since Jamison had blown up at her about going out with Tommy. She needed to talk to him. If nothing else, they needed to get some things straight so they could keep working together. Caite had never been the sort of woman to let things like this slide. It had earned her a lot of heat from past lovers who hadn't appreciated her honesty or forthrightness, but...Jamison was unlike any of them had ever been.

He was different.

The thought of that alone was enough to get her moving. Her bare thighs rubbed together above the tops of her stockings, and the click-click of her high heels on the hallway's tile floor tickled her eardrums. He'd be able to hear her coming.

She knocked on his door and waited for him to reply before opening it. She didn't bother with peeking around the doorframe. She walked right in and closed the door firmly behind her, making sure to lock it.

"We need to talk," she said.

He looked as wary as she felt but nodded and gestured to the chair in front of his desk. Caite took a seat, sitting on the edge. Back straight. Hands folded on her lap. Not sure what she meant to say until the words came out.

"I've had seven lovers in my life," she began without preamble. "A few one-night stands. Two of them were what I might consider serious, long-term. None of them ever, ever did for me what you've done. I'd never asked it of any of them, not outright, though in retrospect I guess there was always that element there. None of them ever responded to me the way you did, Jamison. None of them ever made me feel the way you did. I thought you should know."

He said nothing for a few seconds, so long she began to wonder if he meant to say nothing at all. Then he cleared his throat. "I was married at twenty-four. It lasted two years. I haven't had a girlfriend since that lasted longer than a year. Most less than that. The women I've dated, including my ex, all seemed really happy to let someone else do all the work. All the heavy lifting, I guess you could say. And I thought I liked that for a long time. Having things my way. Getting what I wanted."

"Most people like getting their own way."

He laughed a little shamefacedly and shook his head. "You can't run a relationship like you run a business deal."

"No," Caite said. "I guess you can't."

There was more silence, less awkward than before. Jamison sat back in his chair. Caite kept her position upright, stiff. Professional. She wasn't ready to relax, not just yet.

"What I said to you was wrong," he said.

Her eyebrows rose.

"About knowing your place." His voice dropped. Regretful. "It was arrogant of me, and it wasn't what I meant. I just… You…Damn."

"I what?" She leaned forward a little bit, her posture softening despite her desire to keep up a cold front.

Jamison looked at her. "You came at me so hard, Caite. You're this little bitty thing, and you have this huge presence."

"You're not used to a girl like me," she said, tilting her head to study him. Her heart thumped a little faster. She couldn't stop herself from grinning, just a little.

"No. I'm definitely not." He paused, his expression hardening. "And I'm sure not used to being…to letting…"

He trailed off, and she didn't push him. They shared more silence. Staring at each other.

"If it helps," she said finally, "I'm not used to a guy like you, either."

"I don't think workplace relationships are appropriate, especially between a boss and employee."

She nodded, not surprised but feeling a pinch in her guts just the same. "I understand."

"What if it doesn't work out?" Jamison continued, stony faced. "Working together could put a whole lot of pressure on things."

Her eyebrows rose again, but only for a second or so. "My last boyfriend broke up with me because I wouldn't do his laundry. He said what use was staying together when he knew he'd never marry me if I couldn't just do it for him?"

"Are you asking me if I'll expect you to do my laundry?"

"I'm pointing out that relationships end for all sorts of dumb reasons. Working together isn't necessarily going to make it harder. Or easier." Caite shrugged. "It just means, maybe, that we'll have to be extra honest with each other, that's all. About what we want and expect. And that's not such a bad thing, is it? To start off being honest?"

"I do get tired," Jamison said after a few more beats of silence she timed by the beating of her heart. "What you asked me before…yes. I get tired."

Her guts tumbled and twisted inside her, but Caite kept

herself calm by breathing in through her nose, out through her mouth. In, out, three, four. "You would like to give up once in a while. Let someone else take control."

He shuddered, and she thought for sure he was going to deny it. Worse, that his lip would curl, that he'd send her from the room. Instead, after a long, long moment, he nodded.

An emotion so fierce she didn't know how to name it leaped inside her. In the next second, at the sight of Jamison's slow, sexy smile, Caite knew what it was. Joy. He licked his lips, never looking away from her.

"And I do my own laundry."

"*Would* you do mine?" she asked, meaning to sound light, but her voice dipped low and husky and raw.

Another hesitation, but something gleamed in his eyes. "Yes. If you wanted me to."

"To my specifications? Exactly?" She kept her hands clasped tight, fingers intertwined.

"Yes."

"And what if you didn't do it the way I wanted it done?"

"I guess," Jamison said after a hesitation, "I'd have to make it up to you."

Her cunt tightened at the thought of it. She swept her lower lip with her tongue and reveled in watching his eyes track the motion. "This is complicated."

"I know."

"And you don't like it," she added. "I understand why."

He nodded.

She got up from her chair and went around the desk, helpless against the impulse to touch him. To put her hands on him. To make him real to her in a way he hadn't been for the past eight months, when he'd been nothing more than a shouting voice and a signature on her paycheck.

"Do you want me to stop?" She cupped his face and tipped it to hers.

"No."

She brushed a kiss against his mouth. "Do you want to make me happy?"

Something shifted and shone in his gaze again—something facile and slippery and uncertain that she could see him visibly struggle to subdue. "Yes. I don't know why. But I do."

Caite's laugh snagged in her throat on something suspiciously like a sob. She kissed him, this time harder. Longer. Her tongue quested inside his mouth, and when he at last sucked hers, she moaned against him. Then she pulled away, breathing hard but standing straight. Shoulders squared. She looked him in the eyes.

"Take me to your place. And show me how much you want to make me happy."

# 7

JAMISON TOOK HER to his place, because she'd told him to. If the size of his apartment impressed her, Caite didn't show it. She shrugged out of her coat inside the front door and tossed it onto a chair, then turned to him.

"Bedroom."

"Upstairs," he said. "The loft."

She laughed. "I never guessed you for a man with a…loft."

"What's wrong with a loft?" Jamison asked, not sure why he was laughing, too, only that no woman had ever both aroused and amused him, lifted him and made him lighter, as Caite did.

"Nothing's wrong with a loft. It's just so artistic."

But she changed her mind a few minutes later when he showed her his loft, which was not an open space looking over the main living area but an enclosed bedroom and bathroom reached by a curving staircase. The loft part of it was a cozy balcony furnished with a couple of chairs and a good reading lamp, along with a heavy cherry bookcase stuffed with all his favorite titles.

"I love it," Caite said, looking at the shelves of books, then at him. "It's everything I thought of you. A loft that's not typical but practical. And lovely. And well loved."

He snorted soft laughter at that last bit. "You know all of me so well."

"Not all of you. Not yet," Caite said with a glance at him over her shoulder as she went into his bedroom. She looked over the bed. "You have a housekeeper?"

"No."

She smoothed the bed. "You make your bed this neatly yourself?"

"Yes," Jamison said, and found another laugh.

It could've made all of this seem silly, that laugh, but when she joined him, all it did was make all of this somehow better. He crossed to her and took her in his arms. He kissed her, wondering if she would pull away or chastise him. If she'd put him in the place of…well, a slave, he guessed, thinking of some of the porn he'd seen but had never really liked.

Nothing Caite had done so far had made him feel less than a man, though, and she melted into his touch now with a small shivering sigh that made his cock twitch. He'd been half-hard all day long, his balls heavy and aching with arousal. When she slipped her hands up his chest to link behind his neck, Jamison did what felt natural—he lifted her up to carry her to the bed, where he laid her down carefully. He moved over her, their kisses getting harder until she nipped at his lower lip.

"Slower," Caite commanded in that low, silky voice that was like a fingertip trailing all the way down his spine to his balls.

Jamison moved his mouth from hers to nuzzle and nibble at her neck. The ridge of her collarbone, exposed by her neckline. The first hint of her breasts. Then he stopped. Didn't move. One knee pressed between her legs, nudging upward, then still.

Caite let out a low, frustrated laugh. "Not that slow."

Then they were laughing again, and it had been so long since he'd laughed in bed with a woman…Hell, had he ever? He nuzzled her again, sliding a hand up to cup her breast. They stayed that way for a few minutes.

She put her lips to his ear. "Get on your back."

He rolled, taking her with him so she straddled him. She opened his belt and button on the pants, then the zipper, working efficiently but stopping to look into his eyes as her hand slipped inside. His straining cock peeked out from the top of his briefs, already slick at the head. He thought if she touched him, he'd embarrass himself like a virgin in the back-seat of his dad's Mustang on prom night. When she curved her hand around him through the fabric of his briefs, he did indeed buck upward with a groan.

Caite moved back, off him. "Take off your clothes."

He couldn't move right away, paralyzed at the loss of her touch, until he forced himself to sit up and shrug out of his shirt. Then, standing, he took off his socks. Pants. At his briefs he paused, thumbs in the waistband, and instead of shuck-ing them off and diving on top of her, he remembered what she'd said. *Slower.*

He went slower.

Caite's smile made it worth it. She sat up on the bed, crook-ing a finger. "Come here."

He did, crawling up the bed toward her, but she held him back by putting her foot on his chest. Her toes curled lightly. He waited, impatient but forcing himself to do it anyway. She sat up and ran a fingertip down his shoulder, across his chest. Tweaked his nipple gently. Then harder.

"Do you like pain, Jamison?"

His laugh was harsher this time. "I don't know."

"Do you want to find out?"

His balls tightened at the thought of it. His cock twitched. "Do you?"

"I've never hit anyone on purpose," Caite whispered, voice shaking just enough to make him want to kiss her again and again, to never stop. "I'm not sure how I feel about it, to be honest."

This surprised him enough to sit back. Jamison swallowed. He didn't want to dwell on what the hell he was doing here with her, what she'd awakened in him. Couldn't think too hard about it or how he'd be an idiot about things, he knew it. But he had to ask her.

"You said nobody'd ever responded to you the way I do."

"No. I mean, yes." She laughed. "Nobody ever has. It's intoxicating."

"But you've done…this…before?"

He was grateful he hadn't had to explain himself in greater detail. She got it right away. Caite shook her head slowly. Solemnly.

"If you mean…take control?" she asked delicately, and he couldn't be sure if he was grateful for her hesitation in giving this a more descriptive name or if he wanted to hear her say it out loud.

"Dominate." Jamison coughed on the word, his cock losing some of its thickness with the word.

"Some things," Caite said quietly, "don't need to be named to enjoy them."

They stared at each other. She smiled, urging his own. Whatever it was, she made him want to do it. To please her. To give to her. To give in.

"I've never—" he began, and she put a fingertip to his lips.

"Shhh. I know. On your back," Caite said. "Hands above your head."

In the past he'd indulged lovers who'd wanted to ride him,

but this was different. This was…everything. When she shimmied out of her panties and straddled him, her skirt pushed to her hips, the stockings sleek against him, his fingers gripped the wooden spindles of his headboard hard enough to make it creak.

"Condom?" she asked matter-of-factly.

"Bedside table…. How did you know I'd…?"

"I was hoping. You'd have been a very sad man if you didn't have anything," she whispered, reaching, the motion putting her delectable breasts within reach of his mouth. She laughed when he made to kiss her there and pulled away with a condom in her hand. "Ah, ah, ah."

In seconds she'd sheathed him. A moment after that, she'd settled herself on him with a groan he echoed. His prick throbbed inside her, and again Jamison feared he might spill. She gripped him with internal muscles, rocking, and again he made the headboard complain.

"Slow," she whispered, and reached to unpin her hair. It tumbled around her shoulders in waves of deep honey-blond, and though he longed to sink his fingers into it, Jamison kept his grip tight on the headboard, just as she'd told him to.

She fucked him slowly, every rock and shift of her bringing him to the edge, only to have the pleasure settle back again. Caite closed her eyes, head tipping back. She hadn't unbuttoned more than a couple buttons on her blouse, just enough to give him a hint of cleavage. She ran her hands over her breasts, then her belly, sliding her fingers between them to stroke her clit as her hips moved faster.

She opened her eyes. "I came so hard when your mouth was on me, do you know that?"

"I'm glad," he found the strength to say.

Caite moved faster, biting her lower lip in concentration.

Her eyes met his, not looking away. He let himself drown in their darkness.

"I want you to feel good, Jamison. The way you made me feel."

"I…do…"

"Tell me how good."

He fucked upward, unable to help it. "Feels so damned good, Caite. I want to come."

"I want you to come," she said. "But not just yet. Let me…."

"Oh, yeah."

She cried out, low and raspy. Her pussy bore down on him, milking him, and he fought to keep himself from finishing, even though the world was tipping from the effort. He wanted to come, but his desire to feel her come around his cock was greater than his need to climax. He watched her ride him, her head tipped back, eyes closed in abandon. She was the most beautiful thing he'd ever seen in that moment, when at last she shook with pleasure and cried out his name. The sound of it triggered him at last, and he finished with a hoarse shout.

She covered him with her body for a few seconds, her hair sweeping over him, before she rolled to the side with a contented sigh. "Damn."

Jamison let go of the headboard finally and rolled onto his side to face her. Tucking her hand under her cheek, Caite smiled at him. With her other hand, she pushed away some hair from his forehead and let her fingertip run down his nose to tap lightly on his lips before she got up and swung her legs over the edge of the bed.

She was…leaving?

"Wait a minute," Jamison said.

She glanced at him over her shoulder, already pinning up her hair again. "Hmm?"

"You can stay."

Caite laughed. "I know I can. But I'm not going to."

He sat up, confused and hating it. "Why not?"

"Because," she said as she leaned to kiss him softly, "you will be a grouch in the morning and we'll have to have some sort of weird discussion about what this is or what we are, and you'll be awkward about us working together. And I just can't deal with it, Jamison. I've just had the best sex of my life, ever, and I'd love to bask in the afterglow, but I know you. You're going to…"

She paused with a low hitch in her breath, the confident woman he'd come to crave fading for a moment before she visibly shook herself into self-assurance again. She looked him in the eyes, cupping his face before letting him go. Stepping out of reach.

"I don't want regret," Caite said. "I couldn't stand it, to be honest. It would kill me."

"I don't regret it." The moment he said it, he knew it was true. "Don't go. Stay here with me."

She eyed him, and he could see that as reluctant as she was to agree, she wanted to. "Jamison…"

He didn't try to reach for her, but he got off the bed and moved close enough that she could touch him if she wanted to. "I'm not a man who takes no for an answer."

Caite lifted an eyebrow but didn't disagree.

"I know what I want and how to get it. It's kind of a thing of mine—"

"I've noticed," she said drily. "You kind of have a reputation."

He smiled. "I want you to stay with me tonight. And in the morning, I'll make you breakfast. Anything you like."

"French toast? With powdered sugar?"

"If that's what you want."

Caite crossed her arms, looking stern. "Do you *have* powdered sugar?"

"No. Or eggs. Or milk. Or bread. But I'll get up early enough in the morning to get to the store before you wake up so I can buy everything I need to make you what you want."

"Is that what a submissive man does?" Caite asked, almost as though she was musing.

"I don't know," Jamison said, and finally took her in his arms to tug her closer for a long, lingering kiss. "But I know it's what I do."

When Jamison Wolfe committed to something, he did it at full speed. It shouldn't have surprised Caite, not after watching him work. But discovering that he was very much the same way at play was still a delight and a wonder and something she was going to need more than a few weeks to get used to, no matter how exciting those weeks had been. She'd had devoted boyfriends who'd bowed to her every whim and aggressive lovers who had fought her on everything. She'd never been with a man who could spend the afternoon completely catering to her every need without ever asking her what she wanted as flawlessly and confidently as if he'd downloaded her personal instruction manual, and then spend the night on his knees in front of her while she ordered him to edge himself to orgasm over and over until only the barest breath of her on his cock sent him over the edge.

The combination was heady and electric, and she couldn't get enough, but…

"Enough," Caite breathed as his fingers slowed inside her. Her orgasm had flooded her entire body that time. Boneless and sated, she sank into the couch cushions and tried to catch her breath.

Jamison kissed her mouth, then got up to pour them both

glasses of orange juice from the carafe on the tray he'd set on the coffee table. He'd made her breakfast, hand-fed her bits of French toast and sausage, then made love to her until they both fell asleep on the thick rug in front of the fireplace. Then he'd woken her with his hands and mouth and brought her to another rousing orgasm, and now he was hydrating her.

She could love this man, Caite thought blearily. The idea of it was enough to make her sit up straight. She took the juice. "Thanks, baby."

Jamison brushed her sweat-damp hair off her forehead and kissed her again. "Have to keep my princess happy."

Caite eyed him. "Princess, huh?"

His answer was a cheeky grin. He'd never called her *mistress*. She hadn't asked him to. She'd thought about asking him to call her *domina* but hadn't done that, either. Yet.

"Sure. You don't like it?"

"It's better than pooky sweetums or something like that," she agreed.

Naked, Jamison got up to adjust the gas-fireplace flames. The view was stunning. Long, lean legs, smooth skin, firm ass. The dimples at the base of his spine sent her heart into palpitations.

"You should always be naked in my presence," Caite said.

"That would make it awkward for our clients," Jamison began as he turned to look at her, and just like that, whatever this had become flared again between them.

Thick and heavy with promise, electric. Volcanic. In three heartbeats he was at her feet, kneeling with that perfect ass resting on his heels, his blue eyes gone dark with desire. His pulse throbbing, matched by hers. He leaned to her as she reached for him, and when he put his cheek against her thigh, her fingers buried deep in the thickness of his hair, Caite had never felt so complete.

He stayed like that for a few seconds only. Then his shoulders heaved with a giant breath. He looked at her, mouth thin.

"What, baby?" she asked. "What is it?"

"This…." He ran his hands up her legs to tuck his fingers beneath her thighs. He shook his head.

There was no question it turned her on to have him on his knees for her, but it unnerved her to see him struggle with it. They'd played a bit over the past three weeks with commands and scenes, things they'd seen in porn. But the pomp and ceremony of what Caite refused to call by a four-letter acronym didn't appeal to either one of them. It had become something both simpler and vastly more complicated than that: Caite asked; Jamison complied.

"I like to make you happy," Jamison said. "I don't know why. I just do."

"You do make me happy."

He shook his head a little, cutting his gaze. "It's more than that, Caite. In the past few weeks, I've felt…free."

Her heart lodged in her throat. She sat up to take his face in her hands and turn it toward hers. She kissed him softly. Then again, a little harder. "Me too."

But he still looked troubled, and she didn't know what to say or do to make that change. They sat that way for a moment longer. Then she traced his eyebrows with her fingertip. The curve of his mouth, which finally turned to a smile.

"Why put a name on this?" she murmured. "What other people do is their own business. What we do is ours. So long as we're both making each other happy, do we have to think too hard about it?"

"I haven't had much experience making people happy," Jamison answered, sort of sourly.

His frown charmed her so much she had to kiss him again. "You're good at it. Trust me."

They were quiet together for a while after that, the sort of easy silence that falls between lovers who don't need words to say how they feel. Her hand smoothed over his hair. His breath blew warm on her skin as he rested his head in her lap. They had to get up, she thought lazily. They had to move, to shower, get dressed. But for now it was enough to stay right where they were.

# 8

THE DAILY LISTS were long and detailed and precise, written in Caite's looping hand with the fountain pen she'd snagged from his desk and taken as her own. Random things. Ridiculous things, sort of, which made them all the more important to him for some reason.

Think of her at a certain time on the clock. Wear a specific tie. Order something particular for lunch delivery. Spend an hour exercising, then treat himself to his favorite beer. Text her a picture of his socks. She was big on pictures of what he was wearing, which was really silly since she could see his clothes at any time. It wasn't the photos themselves, Caite had told him, whispering in the darkness with her hand idly stroking his cock and stopping just before he came, so that he'd been floating in a haze of arousal he thought might kill him—and that he'd gladly die from. It wasn't the photos but the fact he was doing it for her because she'd asked it of him. No matter what it was. She liked making the lists because she said it meant he'd be thinking about how to please her all day long. Like foreplay for hours.

As if he wouldn't be thinking about her all day anyway,

Jamison thought. Caite had captivated him. Intoxicated him. He was…addicted.

He thought he might even be in love.

They hadn't talked about that. Not about love or even what this was between them. With Elise out of the office and Bobby settled in his desk down the hall, it would've been so easy for Jamison and Caite to sneak their private life into the work-place. He'd thought about it, of course. That first day in her office when she'd ordered him to go down on her haunted him, sending him a few times to the men's room to force his dick into submission with a cold-water face dunk. Their days at work, however, by unspoken mutual agreement, might simmer with sexual tension because of the lists and the simple fact that with every look they set each other on fire, but they kept themselves as professional as possible.

At least, as much as he hated to admit it, with the *Treasure House* clients bringing Wolfe and Baron more attention and new clients every day, it was easier to keep themselves busy and focused on the job and not each other than it might've been even a few months ago. And it wasn't as if they didn't have any time together away from the job. Three or four nights a week, she came to his place, and their nights were taken up with getting to know each other in every way it was possible for two people to do it. He'd have been glad for more, but Caite had been firm about keeping things professional in the office. She said they needed their time and space away from each other, especially since they worked together. And she was right. She was right about most things he needed or wanted, even if he didn't know it himself.

Or wouldn't admit it. She was good at that, too. Finding all his secrets, even ones he himself hadn't known he had. In only a few short weeks, Caite Fox had turned him inside out.

Jamison scanned the new list she'd left for him that morning before she'd left to do a few site visits. Today's was shorter than usual. One task only.

"Surprise me with something that shows you know me."

For a moment, stumped, Jamison stared at the words on the paper. Caite had proven herself to know him, time and time again, in ways he'd never failed to find amazing. It didn't shock him that she might want him to know her a little, too. The question was going to be, could he do it?

"So you see," Caite said as she demonstrated, "You have to keep your finger pressed to the screen to record. You only get a few seconds. And then the video records, and it makes a loop."

Margeurite Miles was one of the leading concert pianists in the country. She'd forged her name as a child prodigy, performing complicated pieces of music even masters found difficult, and had continued her career by creating an image of herself as something beyond the stereotypical classical musician. Her shows were full of theatrics and special celebrity guests, air cannons of confetti or bubble machines.

She was also technologically incompetent.

"Like this?" Mags held up her phone, a brand-new model she'd brought into Caite's office without even taking it out of the box.

"No…you have to hold in the…Press on the…" Caite demonstrated.

Mags tried again. And failed. But she didn't get frustrated, which was a quality Caite appreciated about her. The older woman wanted to reach out to her younger audience, and if that meant Connex and Buzzvid and Twitter, by golly, she was going to learn how to do it.

Caite had already gone over how to schedule social media updates and some basic training, but so far Mags was simply not getting it. With a sigh, Caite shook her head. Mags laughed, embarrassed.

"I'll practice." Mags held up both hands, wiggling her fingers. "I'm supposed to be good with my hands."

Caite laughed and patted her on the shoulder. "You'll get the hang of it, I'm sure."

"Is our time up?" Mags peered at her phone. "Darn, is the time even right on this thing?"

"The time should almost always be right on that because it's supposed to update automatically. Even if you change time zones." Caite slid a checklist of phone apps and websites across the desk. Normally she'd have emailed it, but Mags never checked her email.

Still, she'd become one of Caite's favorite clients. Helping Mags reach and entertain a new audience felt good. As Caite showed the older woman out, Mags shuffled in her purse, pulling out an envelope.

"This is for you. Two tickets to one of my shows." Mags looked at her. "You have a date, right?"

"I think I can find one."

"If not, I have a really handsome nephew about your age," Mags began as they walked down the hall, only to be interrupted by Jamison coming out of his office. "Oh, Mr. Wolfe. Hello!"

"What's this about tickets to your show?"

Caite held up the envelope. "Mags gave us two tickets. She's trying to set me up with her nephew. Think I can get a better offer than that?"

"My nephew is very handsome," Mags said again, "though... now that I think about it, he's not very funny. Takes after my sister that way, which is really too bad. A man who makes you laugh is a keeper."

"I think we can find you someone who can make you

laugh," Jamison said with a straight face, his gaze piercing Caite's.

Mags waved a hand as she headed for the lobby, leaving them both behind. "Just so long as he doesn't make you cry!"

Caite watched her go, waiting until Mags had turned the corner before facing him. "You do make me laugh."

"Good." He pulled her close for a kiss, nuzzling her neck until she gasped and pushed him away.

"You're the one who said we had to be discreet in the office," Caite muttered, shaking a finger. "Though I'm sure Bobby's got his suspicions."

"Nobody's here to see us. Mags was your last client of the day. And I told Bobby that once she was gone, he could knock off early, too." Jamison bent to nuzzle her again.

Caite held him off and took a step back, out of reach. Since Jamison had been so adamant in the beginning about workplace relationships, she'd made sure to keep any sort of physical hanky-panky to a minimum. Partly to assuage him. Partly to frustrate him. It had been delicious.

"So you think that you're going to get lucky in the office? Is that it? A little afternoon delight?"

"A guy can dream, can't he?" He flashed her a charming grin that threatened to melt her panties, though she didn't so much as bat an eyelash to show him how hot she thought it was.

"Did you finish the list I gave you this morning?"

And just like that, the inferno that constantly simmered between them flared to life.

"I did. Come with me."

His grin, wide and bright, made Caite melt, mostly because she'd seen him smile at a lot of people, and he didn't look at anyone the way he looked at her. No man had ever looked at her the way Jamison did. It didn't only set her on fire. It made her feel adored. Cherished.

Loved.

Which scared her, but she wasn't going to think about that now. Instead she followed him into the conference room, where she let out a small gasp at what lay in front of her. She turned to him, stunned.

"You…did this? All of this?"

His smile was her answer. Caite took an unsteady step toward him, not sure if she meant to laugh or cry. *Surprise me,* she'd told him. He'd done more than that. He'd blown her mind.

Jamison had set the table with a vase of crimson roses in a crystal vase tied with a thick purple ribbon. The flowers were standard—any woman might love red roses—but the ribbon… that was all Caite. Two plates of thin china, matching the ones she had in her apartment, held thick slices of cherry cheesecake. Her favorite. Two wine glasses filled with red wine. A platter of savory crackers and sliced cheeses, along with small bowls of Greek olives.

"Cheesecake for dinner?"

"Dessert first, because you're the sort of woman who breaks the rules," he said. "And just a little appetizer. Dinner reservations are for later, at Serrano. And tickets to see that guy you like. The one who plays the guitar."

Caite couldn't move. She tried to breathe and found the best she could manage was tiny sips of air. She was going to burst into tears, and she didn't want to do that. She swallowed her emotions around the lump in her throat and opened her mouth to thank him.

"There's more," he said before she could say a word. "Open the box."

She'd missed the sleek black box, about the size of a cereal box, though made of much heavier cardboard. Another purple ribbon was tied around it in a crisp bow. Caite went around the table to look at it.

Jamison followed her. "Open it."

All at once, she didn't want to. Her hands shook so much she had to fist them, hiding them in the folds of her full skirt. She couldn't look at him. He'd done so much, all of it proving he knew her exactly. Whatever was in this box would be more of the same or a disappointment, and Caite was suddenly terrified of being disappointed.

"Jamison," she said, but couldn't make herself continue.

He fit himself along her body from behind, his hands slipping around her to press flat on her belly and pull her against him. His kiss found the smooth curve of her neck and shoulder. He didn't nuzzle or try to feel her up. He held her. Offering her his warmth. His support, though he couldn't possibly know her reason for hesitating. Could he?

"I'm scared to open it," she whispered.

"Don't be scared."

"What if I don't like it, whatever it is?"

His gaze, dark with desire, softened. "You wanted me to surprise you. To show I know you. I'm doing the best I can."

"And so far, everything…is perfect." She twisted in his arms to kiss him.

"Shouldn't I be the one who's worried if you won't like it?" His tone was light, but she saw a hint of seriousness in his eyes. "What if I failed?"

"What if you didn't?" Caite asked. "What if you got it just right, because you know me so well?"

Something was changing between them, right there in that moment. Caite could feel it. So could Jamison—she saw it in his eyes and heard it in the catch of his breath. She felt it in his mouth on hers, firm yet somehow searching.

"Open the box, Caite. Please."

So she did.

Jamison didn't imagine her sigh of relief when she undid the ribbon and lifted the box's lid to reveal a matching bra, panty and garter belt set of black lace and emerald-green satin. Caite lifted the scanty underthings from their nest of crumpled tissue paper, along with the pair of sheer nude stockings. The salesgirl had assured him the nude was better than black— Caite was almost certain to already have several sets of black stockings but might need a neutral pair. It had been a bunch of technical jargon to Jamison, but the girl in the shop had convinced him.

"You know my size," Caite said.

"That was the easy part." Jamison watched her stroke the material. She was smiling. That was a good sign. "But there's more."

She looked up at him, then set aside the lingerie carefully on the table. She pulled aside the tissue paper. His stomach lurched, waiting for her to discover what else he'd bought. Two items, chosen even more carefully than the stockings.

Caite pulled out the first and gave a delighted laugh as she held up the red satin and let it run through her fingers. At first she held it to her throat, but before he had to explain what the scarf's true purpose was, she figured it out. Snapping it taut between her fists, she held it up.

"A blindfold." She sounded pleased and, yes, surprised. Something like tears glinted in her eyes for a second before she blinked them away. "How naughty."

"There's one more thing."

Brushing the satin against her lips for a second before putting it aside, Caite nodded. This time, when she found the final item, she gasped. Mouth open, she stared at him for a few seconds before getting herself under control. She pulled her hand out of the box and held up what she'd brought out with her.

Jamison had never been in a sex-toy shop before this morning, when he went in to fulfill Caite's list. The rows of dildos and vibrators hadn't turned his head. Nor had the selection of fetish wear, most of it cheaply made. She was worth more than a catsuit that would split at the seams the first time she wore it. He'd about given up, but then in the back room, a separate section of the store run by a different vendor who was renting space, he'd found what he was looking for. Handcrafted of smooth, supple leather. No buckles, but instead thin silk cord wound through punched holes. The cuffs were unique and beautiful, just like Caite.

But they weren't for her.

"Jamison," she said in a low voice, letting her fingers toy with the cords that closed the cuffs. "Oh, my God. Oh."

Sewn into the leather's edge were genuine pearls, three on each cuff. He could've special-ordered them with other jewels, diamonds, rubies. Embroidered with his name or hers. But the moment Jamison had seen the pearl-edged cuffs, he'd known they were the ones.

Caite brought them to her face and sniffed, eyes closed. "I love the smell of leather. I love pearls."

"I know."

"These are gorgeous," she murmured, holding the cuffs to her cheek for a second or so before looking at him. "And unexpected. I mean, completely not at all what I was expecting. You really surprised me."

When Jamison was closing in on the end of a deal, his world shifted. Vision narrowed. When he had the other guy in his sights, everything going the way he wanted it to, the guarantee of success became so close he could taste it, thick like honey but sweeter. In those moments, winning, he felt as though he were in a different universe. He felt that way now, too, though instead of sweetness, an anxious bitterness teased his tongue.

"You'd like to use them on me," he said aloud. He didn't stutter or stumble; the words came out of him with as much confidence as anything he'd ever said while sealing a negotiation. On the inside, though, everything had gone dark and swimming. Uncertain. "You'd like to bind my hands, Caite. You'd like to get me on my knees with my hands behind my back, using those cuffs."

A slow creeping flush eased up her throat to paint her face. She licked her lips, and the sight of her tongue moving across them sent a wave of desire flooding straight to his already half-hard cock. She stroked the leather again, then the shimmering, creamy pearls.

"And they don't lock," she said under her breath, almost as though she were talking to herself. "You'd be bound more by my desire than by the cuffs themselves. Oh, fuck, Jamison. Oh, God, I love them. But will you?"

Of everything they'd done, her desire to control him in this way had been the one thing he'd felt certain he'd deny her if she asked. The lists, the commands, the hours he'd spent worshipping her body before ever even getting close to achieving his own release—all of that had seemed like something from a dream. If you'd asked him months ago if he'd ever submit sexually to a woman in that way, Jamison might've laughed or even thrown a punch, depending on who was doing the asking. Nothing Caite had asked of him had ever felt cheap or abusive or castrating. But this...

"It's crossing the line," he said.

Caite nodded, then tilted her head to study him. Her eyes

were bright, her mouth lush and moist. The quickness of her breathing was echoed in the rise and fall of her shoulders.

"You're not sure about it," she told him. "I understand. And I don't want to ever force you into something you don't like. But you bought these for me. You knew how much I would love them even though I've never asked this of you. You knew it anyway."

"Yes."

"This, between us. It's not a game," Caite whispered, moving closer. "Is it?"

"No, Caite." He kissed her. Hard. Taking it, not asking for it or waiting for permission. His thoughts were rough-and-tumble, his conflicting desires fighting with each other. He didn't want this to be a game.

But what did he want, exactly?

"Take off your clothes," Caite said in a firm, low voice. She put a hand between them to hold off another kiss.

He could've refused her, but then, that was what turned them both on so much, wasn't it? That he should have all the power. Bigger, stronger…her boss, for fuck's sake. But he gave it up to please her, and she took it to please them both.

Jamison loosened his tie and tugged it free. He took off his jacket and laid it over a chair. Then opened his shirt buttons, one by one, and added his shirt to the pile. His cock had begun to strain at his pants, and when he slipped out of them, the bulge in his briefs drew Caite's gaze.

"Hold," she said in that voice, the darker tone that got him rock hard in seconds. "I want to admire you for a minute."

And she did, walking all around him in a circle, occasionally touching him. A light drift of fingers from shoulder to shoulder along his collarbone, then down his center line to the first hint of hair leading into his briefs. Her touch tickled but aroused.

"So beautiful," she told him.

His first instinct was to bristle. *Beautiful* was a word for women. But when she stopped in front of him to look up at him, no hint of mockery in her gaze, only appreciation, Jamison relaxed into Caite's adoration.

"Take off the briefs."

He did, slowly, adding a little bump and grind to make her laugh. She did, breathlessly. Her eyes shone.

"Put this on." She handed him the blindfold. He tied it over his eyes.

He stood in front of her naked, cock so hard it tapped his belly when he moved. With the blindfold on, every other sense became slowly heightened. He remembered that first night with her. How she'd urged him to let go and how, though it went against everything he'd ever done, he had.

"I never thought," Caite breathed into his ear, "how much I needed this until you gave it to me."

The leather was smooth on his wrists. When she touched his hands, he put them automatically behind him, crossed at the base of his spine. His heart thundered in his ears. His breath grew short. Once he did this, once he gave in to her this way...

"Crossing the line." Her voice teased his ear again. Her lips brushed it. Her touch, gentle but firm, shackled him. "Oh, Jamison, you have made me so, so happy."

That made it worth it. To be naked and bound in the conference room where he was usually the king, to make her the queen, instead. Whatever she wanted to do, he was willing to let her. When she told him to get on his knees, he did. Because he...

"Are you okay?" Caite's whisper, coming from the side opposite of where she'd been, startled him. "I'm not going to hurt you."

He tensed, swallowing against a dry throat. "I know."

"What are you thinking, sweetheart?"

It was the perfect time to tell her that he wanted to make this something permanent between them. Not an office affair they had to hide. It was the perfect time to tell her that he loved her.

But then the creak of the office door alerted him that they weren't alone.

"Holy shit, sorry," came Tommy's familiar voice. "Sorry, Caite. Shit, I was just driving past and wanted to see if you'd come with us…"

*Us. Shit.* Jamison was on his feet, unable to tear at the blindfold or do a fucking thing with the cuffs on his wrists. He yanked, feeling the silk cord give, thanking every fucking god that would listen and even the ones that wouldn't that he hadn't bought the ones with metal buckles.

"Get out," Caite said, but it was too late.

"Hey, look at that," came Nellie's voice, full of giggles. Which meant Paxton was right behind her. "Wow!"

"Sorry," Tommy said again, and Jamison wanted to rip the guy to shreds. "Nellie, get the hell out of here. This isn't your business."

Caite's hands were on him, but Jamison shrugged away from her touch, turning, furious and ashamed. He yanked again on the cuffs, hard enough to worry that he might break something in his wrists before he broke the cord. His struggle had loosened them enough, though, so that he could peel one off. He ripped at the blindfold and tossed it down. Breathing hard, feeling sick, he started grabbing at his clothes without looking to see who was still there.

Caite stood alone, looking as disgusted as he felt. She said his name, but he held up a hand to keep her from saying anything else. He pulled on his clothes, not taking the time to be neat or tidy with it, just desperate not to be naked any longer.

One cuff still dangled from his wrist, keeping him from putting his shirt on. He tore it free and tossed it onto the table. Caite stared at it. Slowly, slowly, she bent to pick up the blindfold he'd thrown to the floor.

"Jamison," she said. "They're gone. Don't do this."

Everything he'd given her, everything he'd been willing to give, rose inside him like vomit. He shook his head. "This isn't me. This isn't who I am."

He was ashamed to see tears sliding down her face, but even when she reached for him, he couldn't let her touch him. He stepped back, out of reach. At this rejection, Caite let her hands fall to her sides.

"We don't have to," she whispered. "If you don't want to do that, it's fine, it's all right—"

"But it's what you want, isn't it?" he shouted, voice hoarse and raw as though he'd been screaming for hours. "It's what gets you off, isn't it?"

"It's what gets you off, too," Caite cried, then, softer, "and it's not something shameful. Do you feel ashamed?"

He said nothing, but he didn't have to. She read it all over him. Caite trembled, biting her lower lip, then closing her eyes as more tears spilled down her face.

"Oh," she said in a small wounded voice. "Well, then."

And after that, nothing more had to be said.

# 9

"THREE WEEKS." ELISE groaned. "Three immortally long, boring weeks until they'll even consider inducing me. If I have to watch another daytime TV show I'm going to explode with boredom. Though I was thinking about that, Caite, taking on some of those clients. Which, by the way, how's it going with the *Treasure House* people?"

Caite's attention had been snagged by the sight of Jamison heading down the hall to his office and passing her door, but now she returned her focus to the computer screen. "Oh… really well. We've managed to get their visibility rating up in the past few weeks. There's a big event scheduled for tonight. I'll be covering that."

"Is Jamison going with you?"

Caite paused. Jamison hadn't said more than a few words to her since the afternoon in the conference room. Almost a month ago. He'd spoken of business when necessary, but any other attempts at getting him to talk to her about what had happened were met with stony silence. They were back to where they'd been in the beginning. He hated her, she thought, for crossing the line.

"I don't think so."

Elise sighed. She looked better than she had the last time Caite had seen her in the office, but her pregnancy was clearly taking its toll. "How's he doing, by the way?"

Caite didn't answer right away, not sure what her other boss was getting at. "Um, fine?"

"I mean, he's letting you do what you have to do, isn't he? He's not being too overbearing?"

A vision of Jamison on his knees, hands behind him, prick proud and ready for her, dried Caite's throat so much she couldn't answer right away. Elise didn't seem to notice. She shook her head.

"If he is, I can talk to him about it. I have every confidence that you're completely competent, Caite. Or else I wouldn't have hired you." Elise paused to take another deep breath. "God, I never thought I'd miss the days of going to the gym. I feel like such a slug."

"Not much longer now," Caite answered. "Before you know it, you'll have a little bouncing bundle of joy to keep you so busy you'll be wishing you could stay in bed."

Elise smiled. "Yes. I can't wait. This event tonight, it's not the usual *Treasure House* scene. How'd you score it?"

"Tommy is a big supporter of the charity that's sponsoring the dinner dance. I get the feeling that the other two couldn't give a rat's ass about it, but they're contractually obligated to all go to the same things. He twisted Pax's arm, and of course, wherever Pax goes, Nellie follows. They got matching tattoos last week. Got a surprising amount of negative commentary on it, too." Caite paused, leaning back in her chair so she could casually strain for a glimpse of Jamison's office door. She looked back at her computer to find Elise giving her a quizzical look. "Anyway, this event's a great way to gain some positive spin on the three of them as well as the show.

Tommy's donating a huge portion of his *Treasure House* prize to the foundation."

"If they win it. Well, it will definitely be good publicity and should lead to some other good opportunities, so long as they behave themselves." Elise yawned. "But I guess that's why you'll be there, in case they don't."

"Damage control," Caite murmured. "That's my job. Fixing things when they've gone bad."

The question was, she thought as she and Elise disconnected their call, would she be able to fix what had gone wrong with her and Jamison?

In a room filled with the light of hundreds of candles, Caite Fox looked luminous. It was the only way to describe her. And Jamison hated it, because he couldn't stop trying to find her with his gaze, no matter where she went in the room.

Three weeks. Three heinously long, tense weeks, since the nightmare of being found in a compromising position had sent him over the edge. He'd seen her every workday after that, of course, but they'd done little more than send each other memos or have Bobby relay messages. The atmosphere in the office had been…tense. At least for him. Caite hadn't seemed to be bothered much by it at all.

He'd been unable to stop thinking about her. Being underneath her. Pleasing her. For the first time since puberty, when he'd started fantasizing about sex, Jamison's dreams hadn't focused on what he was going to do *to* a woman but rather what he could do *for* her. And nothing seemed to ease the ache.

"Hey, man." Tommy clapped a hand on Jamison's shoulder. "Thanks for coming out."

The kid had cleaned up pretty good, Jamison noted. Suit, no tie, but his long hair had been tied at the nape of his neck with a cord. A faint pattern of bruising on his cheek made him a little less pretty. Jamison still wanted to match it on the other side with his fists.

Instead, he forced a grin. If the little prick intended on making something out of what he'd seen, he'd have Jamison to answer to, client or not. "Part of my job."

Tommy laughed but as if they were buddies, not as if he were making fun. "I hope we can count on a donation from you anyway. At least bid on something from the silent auction."

Jamison turned to look him in the eyes. "This foundation, it means a lot to you."

"I lost my kid sister to Creutzfeldt–Jakob disease. There isn't much known about prion disease. If I can help out, even a little…" Tommy shrugged. The two men stood in awkward silence for a minute before Tommy spoke again. "She's a prize, you know. Caite. She's the kind of woman I would do anything for. Am I right?"

Jamison clenched his fists, though halfheartedly. The kid was right, after all. "I bet you would."

"Damned right I would. And be glad of the chance to make her my queen…but you know something about that, don't you?" Tommy took a step back as though expecting Jamison to lunge at him. Not as if he were scared by the thought. More as if he was being cautious.

"Look. I don't give a flying fuck what you think," Jamison began, but cut himself off when Tommy held up a hand.

"I get it, man. I get it more than you could possibly imagine. And I envy you. The way she looked at you…I won't lie. I'd give up anything to be able to give it up to her."

Jamison was silent.

Tommy lifted his chin toward the crowd in front of them. "You think any other woman out there can give you what she can? Be the woman you need, deep down in your soul?

Because if your answer's anything other than no, I'm going to take her from you. If she'll have me."

For a second or so, it felt as though the floor physically tilted, but it was only his equilibrium. Jamison's lip curled. "You could try, I guess."

"Wouldn't have to try too hard, would I?" Tommy gave Jamison a wicked grin. "Seeing as how you're just standing there, letting her go."

In the next moment, Tommy was tugged away by a fawning woman who'd earlier given Jamison his raffle ticket. Jamison watched them go, feeling a lot more respect for the reality star than he had before. With a quick check of the social media stream, reassured that Caite's handiwork of timed updates was doing its job, he headed for the small room off the main banquet hall where the silent auction had been set up. There was the usual—handcrafted baskets filled with soaps or wine or chocolate. Gift certificates to local spas or for holiday home rentals. But there, off to the end, was something he wanted the moment he saw it.

"Pretty, huh," Caite said quietly.

"Gorgeous."

She meant the necklace, a single strand of creamy antique pearls displayed on a velvet mat. He meant her. But he kept his eyes on the necklace and the sign-up sheet. The bidding had already gone over $200, still an insanely cheap price for real pearls.

"They're vintage," she said. "Came from an estate. They're not farmed pearls, either—you can see how they're not exactly matched."

He let his gaze drift to her. "You know a lot about pearls."

"Not really. Just what I like." She looked at him, finally, her gaze warm but not intimate.

It pinched at him, the way she let it slide away from him as

CROSSING THE LINE

though he'd never feasted on her pussy and tasted her coming on his tongue. "I always figured you more for a diamond sort of woman. Pearls seem soft."

Her eyebrows rose. "I didn't figure you spent any time at all thinking about what sort of woman I was. At all. Or what I like."

With that, she stalked off, and Jamison watched her go before shaking himself into action. He followed her from the ballroom to snag her elbow, bared by her sleeveless gown. Her skin, warm beneath his fingertips, was smooth as silk. He turned her. He was gripping too hard, he saw when she winced a little and tried to pull away from him. He let her go.

"Caite. I want to talk to you."

He didn't miss the way she looked all around them before meeting his eyes again. "About?"

"Just come with me." Before she could protest, he'd taken her by the elbow again to hustle her down a short hallway used by the waitstaff. By the time they got to a small alcove by the elevators, she'd tugged herself free of him.

She turned to face him. "What's going on? Is it something with the clients? Because Nellie and Paxton have actually been on their best behavior at this thing, and Tommy is…"

"No," Jamison said. "It's not about them. Your handling of things has been…exemplary."

"Ah." She leaned against the wall with her hands flat on it next to her. "So. What, then?"

He kissed her.

Long and hard and fierce, one hand sliding beneath the fall of her sleek blond hair to cup the back of her neck. For a second or so, he thought he'd severely misjudged, but when she whimpered into his open mouth and put her arms around him, he bent back to the kiss with added fervor. They ate of each other, mouths and hands and moans all together. When he broke, gasping, to breathe, Caite wound her arms around him and pulled him back in.

"We could do this forever," he said after another few minutes of her mouth making him crazy. "But we should do it somewhere else."

Caite blinked, the haze in her eyes fading. She smiled a little. "Is that what you want?"

"I want you," he said in a low, growling voice he barely recognized. Everything about her made him crazy....No, he thought as she stepped out of his arms to straighten her dress and smooth her hair. To wipe at the corners of her mouth where his kiss had smeared her lipstick. Being without her had made him lose his mind. Being with her again had made him sane.

She looked over his shoulder at the passing waiter heading back toward the ballroom. "I have work to do, Jamison."

"After."

Caite paused, letting her tongue slide over her lower lip. "I don't know."

He took two steps back from her. His fists balled; she saw it but didn't look scared. Her gaze flickered. Again, the swipe of her tongue across her lips. The hitch of her breath made him think that while she was playing at being reluctant, she might actually want him, too.

"After the banquet and dancing," she said slowly. "Then we can talk."

He nodded. Neither of them moved. Caite tipped her chin up, her hands flat again on the wall, one on either side of her thighs. She turned her head slowly, slowly, exposing the line of her neck and throat to him. It drew him, moth to flame, bee to flower.

"No," she breathed when he moved closer. "After."

Caite had heard the term *weak in the knees* but had never understood it until now. She'd waited until Jamison had gone, leaving her near that elevator, before she'd let out the breath she'd been holding. She'd had to hold on to one of the stacked chairs along the wall and force herself to drag in breath after breath to keep herself from dropping to her hands and knees to stop the world from spinning. It had taken every bit of strength she'd had to keep herself from climbing him like a tree right then and there.

After, he'd said, and she had agreed.

But what would that mean? After the dinner, which she couldn't bring herself to eat. After the dancing, which had just begun. And then what? What could they possibly have to say to each other? she wondered as she returned to the ballroom.

"Great night." Tommy was well known for his taciturn nature, but just now he was beaming. He looked around the room, catching sight of Nellie and Paxton holding court, and if it annoyed him, he barely let it show. He put an arm around Caite's shoulders, easing her closer to say into her ear, "Thanks for all your support, Ms. Fox. Without Wolfe and Baron, and really, mostly you, this event wouldn't have had half the attention it's been getting. Online donations have doubled."

"It's a good cause." She slipped an arm around his waist for a second to squeeze him in return.

He looked at her. "The foundation wasn't your client—I was. But even so, you really went above and beyond. I recommended they take a look at hiring you for some future events. It's nonprofit, so I'm not sure what their budget is…."

"We do pro bono work for a few different places. I'm sure I can work with them." She gave a satisfied sigh, looking around, trying not to act as if she was looking for Jamison.

"He's over by the silent-auction stuff." Tommy laughed, leaning closer again to whisper into her ear. "But dance with me first."

She eyed him. "What makes you think I was looking for him?"

"He's the boss, right? Making sure it all goes okay. Boss man." Tommy laughed and shook his head. He offered her his hand.

She took it, letting him lead her to the dance floor, where he settled his hands easily on her hips and led her into a few simple steps. They talked as easily as they danced—Tommy was passionate but also well educated about the disease for which he'd spent so much effort raising money, and Caite admired both his enthusiasm and his knowledge.

"We're going to start calling out the winners of the silent auction. Feel free to keep dancing! Winners, if your name's called, come on up to the front here to get your item." The voice from the front of the room echoed a little through the mic. The silent auction signaled the end of the night.

"You know, there's a lot more to you than meets the eye," she said.

Tommy laughed and spun her slowly out, then in for a dip. "I could say that about a lot of people. You, for example."

"Me?" Caite pretended surprise. "Like what?"

But before he could answer, a big male hand came down on his shoulder. "Can I cut in?"

Tommy laughed and nodded, graciously stepping out of the way so Jamison could take his place. When he had, Jamison looked down at Caite with what had become a familiar heat blazing in his eyes. "I didn't like the way he was handling you. You know you don't have to let him, right? Just because he's a client?"

Caite frowned, looking past him to where Tommy was now standing for photos with Nellie and Pax. "It wasn't a hardship, Jamison."

Jamison said nothing in reply. Not with words. His expression said it all, and though she kept hers carefully neutral in response, inside she warmed. She moved herself a little closer, into his arms, tipping her head back to look at his face.

"You're protective," she murmured.

"I wanted to make sure he wasn't bothering you."

"You wanted to make sure no other man was touching me," Caite said.

She hadn't known for sure it was the truth until she saw his reaction, a thinning of his mouth. Narrowed eyes. And, against the front of her, the sudden press of his erection. She smiled and looked away from him to keep herself from jumping into his arms and feasting on his mouth.

"We can go now," Caite said, already thinking about the promise of "after" and what it meant. Her nipples went tight. Her pussy tensed. The heat in her stomach kindled higher. Hotter, rising to her throat.

"Not just yet."

Curious, she looked at him, just as the voice that had been calling out the winners' names for the past ten minutes said very clearly, "Caitlyn Fox! Congratulations—you won the set of antique pearls, generously donated by one of our volunteer coordinators! Please come to the back of the room to get your prize."

Caite shook her head. "I didn't—"

"I did," Jamison said.

# 10

THEY WERE GORGEOUS. The most beautiful piece of jewelry Caite had ever owned. The most expensive, too. She'd made no protest at the banquet when Jamison had slipped them around her throat, but here in his apartment, standing in front of him, she couldn't stop herself from being honest.

"You didn't have to do this, Jamison."

"I wanted to," he said, turning with a glass of whiskey in his hand, the bottle in the other.

"You can't…buy me," Caite said.

For a moment, he only stared at her. Then he put the glass down. The bottle. He crossed to her in three long strides and took her by the arms, hard enough to hurt. Her heart lodged in her throat, pounding, and only half in fear.

"Is that what you think I'm trying to do?"

"I don't know what you're trying to do," she told him. "I don't have any idea about you. Who you are. What you want. I thought I did, but I was wrong."

"You weren't wrong," Jamison said, and went silent.

Caite waited for him to speak, but when he didn't, she sighed and briefly pressed her fingertips to the inside corners of her eyes. For a moment, her shoulders slumped as she fought to find the words she wanted—no, needed—to say. She looked up at him at last, desperate to see something in his face that would let her know what he was thinking, what he wanted from her. For them. But all she saw was a faintly neutral expression. Maybe he was waiting, too.

But there was nothing much she could say other than the truth. "I'll be tendering my resignation on Monday. I've been offered the chance to represent Tommy's foundation on a permanent basis. Media campaign planning. That sort of thing. It's not in violation of my noncompete agreement. I checked with Elise already."

She'd been expecting a few different reactions but not this one. Jamison growled. Then came at her like…well, like a wolf running down a deer. Except that Caite wasn't running. She stood her ground when he grabbed her. Didn't even tremble when he crushed his lips to hers.

"No," he said against her mouth. "You're too damn good at the business. Wolfe and Baron can't afford to lose you, Caite."

Everything inside her wanted to explode, but she kept herself very, very still. Jamison buried his face against her neck. Holding her. The embrace softened, and finally, she put her arms around him.

"No," he said again.

She pushed him gently until she could look at his face. "Sit."

He did, in the oversize leather armchair in front of the fireplace, but pulled her onto his lap. She didn't protest. She snuggled against him for a moment, listening to the sound of his breathing.

"Elise isn't coming back to work," Jamison said. "She's decided to stay home, do some consulting for us on a part-time basis. But mostly stay home after the baby's born."

"She didn't say anything about that when I talked to her," Caite began, but Jamison cut in.

"I talked to her. And we agreed that we wanted to ask you to join the company as a partner. Wolfe, Baron and Fox. We were going to talk to you about it together, but…"

Caite laughed without much humor. "I told you, Jamison. You can't buy me."

"This isn't about buying you!" he shouted, then softened his tone immediately. "I'm sorry, Caite, I didn't mean to shout. Please. Listen to me. I don't want you to quit. I don't want you to leave. I don't want you to leave *me*."

Hope, the most dangerous of emotions.

"I want to believe you. But I don't know you," she said finally. "I thought I did, but I don't. At least, you don't seem to want what I can give you."

Jamison shifted her on his lap. "What I want is you. Hell. Quit the business, don't take a partnership. I don't care. Just give me another chance."

She laughed at that and made to get up, but he held on to her just hard enough to change her mind. "You're ashamed of us, Jamison. Of what we do together. And part of me understands that, because it was all new to me, too. But the other part of me doesn't get it, because when I was with you, I never felt like I was crossing a line. I just felt…good. Happy."

"I did, too. What can I do to make you believe me?"

As she looked into his eyes, believing him was all she wanted to do. "I don't know."

Jamison frowned. They sat together that way for another minute or so, until at last she cuddled against him, tucking her head into the curve of his shoulder. They breathed together, in and out, in perfect sync. She put her hand on his chest to feel the thumping of his heart.

"I was wrong," Jamison said finally. "I was proud and

wrong, and, yes, I was ashamed. It's hard, you know. To let go. And to have someone see it…I was embarrassed."

"I know." She nuzzled his throat, letting her tongue taste him for a second or so. Underneath her, she felt him stir, and it made her smile despite herself.

He sat back to look at her face. "Can you forgive me?"

"You're not a man who's used to apologizing." She thought on that for a second. "Thank you. And yes. Of course I can forgive you."

"Can you forget, though?" He smiled a little.

"No." Caite shook her head. "I can't do that. But I can look past it. I can let it be unimportant."

Jamison nodded. "If that's the best I can hope for, I'll take it."

"That's not negotiation," Caite said sternly. "You can do better than that."

Then they were laughing together, slow rolling giggles that surged up and out of them both until the air rang with them. And then they were kissing, over and over again. Hands roaming. He was hard and she was straddling him, cupping his face in her hands. How could she ever have thought she wouldn't give him a second chance?

"I want more than four nights a week with you," Jamison said. "In return, I offer breakfast every morning."

"Done. But you have to give me half the closet space," she told him. "And never, ever use my toothpaste. And I will not use your razor for my legs, even if I don't have one."

"Agreed. So…we have a deal?" he asked, giving her a wicked grin. "Do we sign the contract?"

Slowly, Caite rocked against his hardness until his fingers tightened on her hips and his lips parted. He got that look in his eyes. And then she said, "Let's just say the negotiations have begun."

Jamison let out a small groan at the press of her against him. "Is this going to be a complicated negotiation?"

"I don't think so," Caite breathed. "I think it's going to be very simple. You do your best to make me happy, and I'll do the same for you."

"I love you," he said. "And I can't promise you I'll always know what to do, but I can promise you I'm always going to give you everything I can."

"I love you, too," Caite said. "And I'll take it."

★ ★ ★ ★ ★

## About the Author

*USA TODAY* bestselling author **Sarah Morgan** writes hot, happy contemporary romance, and her trademark humor and sensuality have gained her fans across the globe. She has been nominated three years in succession for a prestigious RITA® Award from the Romance Writers of America and has won the award twice, in 2012 and 2013. She also won the RT Reviewers' Choice Award in 2012 and has made numerous appearances in their Top Pick slot.

Sarah lives near London with her family, and when she isn't reading or writing she loves being outdoors, preferably on vacation so she can forget the house needs tidying.

Readers can find out more about Sarah and her books from her website, www.sarahmorgan.com. She can also be found at www.facebook.com/authorsarahmorgan and on Twitter: @SarahMorgan_.

**Books by Sarah Morgan**

**Cosmo Red-Hot Reads from Harlequin**

RIPPED

**Harlequin HQN**

SLEIGH BELLS IN THE SNOW
SUDDENLY LAST SUMMER (July 2014)

**Harlequin Presents**

LOST TO THE DESERT WARRIOR
AN INVITATION TO SIN
SOLD TO THE ENEMY

# BURNED

## Sarah Morgan

Dear Reader,

Do you have a relationship in your past you think about? Ever wondered what would happen if that guy walked through your door again? Rosie, the heroine of *Burned,* is about to find out!

I first introduced Rosie in *Ripped,* and the moment I hinted at a past relationship gone bad, I knew I wanted to explore her story in more depth. Karate champion Rosie has a close relationship with her sister and loves her job as a fitness instructor in a big city gym. She's a typical *Cosmo* girl, fearless and fun-loving, and when it comes to defending herself no one has more experience than Rosie. She's been defending her heart since the age of eighteen, when she fell in love with martial arts expert Hunter Black. That relationship scarred her so badly she won't even allow his name to be mentioned, so when he walks back into her life, she knows she's in trouble, and it doesn't help that the chemistry between them is hotter than ever.

Rosie will let him back into her bed, but will she let him back into her heart?

I hope you enjoy *Burned!*

Love,

Sarah xx

# 1

HE WAS BREAKING up with me.

I shouldn't have minded. I should have been used to it after all the experience I'd had, and it wasn't as if I were in love or anything—do I look stupid?—but every girl likes to think she's irresistible and being dumped hurts, especially after the day I'd had at work.

There is nothing worse than every part of your life going wrong at the same time. You see the whole thing unravelling and you don't know which bit to grab.

'The thing is, Rosie, this just isn't working out. We're not compatible. You're not very—' he squirmed in his seat 'you know...'

No, I didn't know, but that was one of the things that annoyed me most about Brian. He never finished his sentences. He stopped before the end and I was supposed to guess the missing words. Of all the infuriating habits I'd ever encountered while dating, not finishing sentences was the most exasperating—and that's from someone who once dated a delightful individual who threw his beer bottle at the bin and missed every time, despite having perfect aim when glued to the Xbox killing aliens. I'm the sort of girl who reads the last page of a book first to check how it ends, so cliffhangers aren't for me. Just give me the bad news and get it over with. Don't make me wait.

I'd blown two weeks' rent on a dress and now it was going to waste. This place was expensive. Right on the river with a view across to the London Eye. I loved the London Eye. It was a fairground ride for grown-ups, a giant Ferris wheel on the South Bank that offered a perfect view of the city. The glass capsules made me think of a monster with big buggy eyes. I wished it would come and gobble up Brian.

I heard laughter coming from the bar area and saw a group of men, shirts unbuttoned at the neck, jackets slung carelessly over the backs of chairs, drinking champagne like soda. It was Friday night and they were office types with money to burn. Lawyers? Bankers?

One of them was watching me. He caught my eye and smiled.

I didn't smile back.

What was there to smile about?

The fitness club where I worked had been bought by a company I knew nothing about, which meant the job I loved was threatened. Who knew what changes the new management would want to make? There had been more rumours than workouts for the past few weeks and the uncertainty was driving me mad. And now my fragile love life had crumbled to dust. All in all it wasn't turning out to be my best week.

Feeling gloomy, I looked away and saw a couple laughing together, lost in each other. The man was handsome, the woman beautiful. His hand sneaked across the table and covered hers, as if he couldn't bear to not be touching her. Her eyes smiled into his. Their wine was untouched. So was their food. They were too wrapped up in each other to notice anything around them, especially not the girl being dumped at the next table. I wanted to step out of my world and join them in their shiny happy place.

Even as I watched, they stood up simultaneously, gazes still locked. I should have looked away, but I couldn't. There was something mesmerizing about the intensity of their chemistry. I stared, fascinated, envious, as the guy threw a bundle of notes on the table without counting them. So cool. I've only ever seen that happen in the movies. If I'd done the same thing I would have showered the table with receipts, expired discount vouchers, chocolate wrappers and a ton of other crap that somehow finds its way into my purse. He strode purposefully to the door, his hand locked in hers. I knew, I just knew, that they weren't going to make it to the car without ripping at each other's clothes. I'd never seen two people so into each other. Or maybe I had. Ever since my sister, Hayley, had got it together with Nico Rossi, the two of them had been like that. I was scared to open the door to our apartment in case I tripped over the pair of them in the hallway. I joked that it made me mildly nauseous, but honestly, I was happy for my sister. Neither of us found relationships easy. I was glad one of us had managed to find someone.

'Rosie? Are you even listening to me?'

I turned back to Brian, telling myself I wasn't jealous. Chemistry that intense was a bad thing. It could scorch a person. I knew. I was much better off sticking with this bland version of a relationship, even if it did fizzle out like a firework on a wet night. Better that than being burned.

'I'm listening. I was waiting for you to finish your sentence. You were telling me we're not compatible.' It was like one of those stupid reality shows where they're about to tell you who this week's loser is, who is going home, only instead of just doing it, they make you wait and wait against the backdrop of a drama drum roll until the whole nation is yelling, 'For fuck's sake, get on with it,' at the TV. To kill time, I glanced round the room. Sleek black tables shimmered with silver and candles. We were surrounded by the low hum of conversation and the clink of glass. A roomful of people enjoying an evening. People who were in relationships.

And then there was me.

Rosie the rejected.

I could hold water in my hands longer than I could hold a man. Not that I wanted a long relationship but hanging on to him until the end of dinner would have been confidence building.

'Look at you....' Brian waved a hand and I looked down at myself in alarm, wondering if I'd had a wardrobe malfunction. We're big on those in my family—just ask my sister, Hayley. But as far as I could see, it was situation normal. Same legs. Same flat chest. When my sister and I were dividing up the family DNA, she got the big-breast gene. Who am I kidding? She got the whole breast gene. All of it. I've always liked to put a positive spin on things, so I told myself a flat chest gave me a better view of my impressive abs. I'd worked hard enough to get them.

'I'm looking. I don't see a problem.'

'There isn't a problem! You're really pretty. Great bone structure, cute face, gorgeous smile and your legs are—' He cleared his throat. 'You've got *great* legs. Great body. It's not the way you look! On the outside you look feminine and fragile, but on the inside you're not....'

'I'm not what? Brian, for the love of all that is holy, *please* finish your sentences.'

'I did.'

'You said "inside you're not." What am I not?'

'You're not at all fragile.' His face was scarlet and the colour didn't suit him. 'There isn't even a hint of vulnerability about you.'

'You *want* me to be vulnerable?' I thought about the mess that lay in my past. I thought about my childhood, when I'd spent half my time feeling vulnerable. Looking back on how I'd been then made me cringe. And he was telling me he wanted me that way?

He finished his food and put down his fork. 'You're tough, Rosie.'

That didn't sound so bad to me. 'So is diamond. And it sparkles.'

'I was thinking more of Kevlar.' He sighed. 'You have to admit your interests are…unusual.'

'What's wrong with my interests?'

'Oh, come on!' His expression said it should have been obvious. 'You're a girl and you like fighting. How do you think that makes me feel?' He glanced quickly to the left to check no one was listening, as if simply being seen with someone like me might be enough to knock lumps off his manhood.

I put my fork down, too. Not because I'd finished eating— being dumped wrecks my appetite—but so I wouldn't be tempted to stab him. 'Martial arts, Brian. You make it sound as if I'm pounding on people in the street.'

'What you do is violent! You kick people. You could kick me.'

I had to rein myself in.

I told myself it wasn't an invitation.

All the same I was tempted.

My shoes had a particularly sharp heel. They deserved a workout before they went back in the box.

A couple had arrived at the recently vacated table. I decided they didn't deserve to have their evening ruined. I glanced idly in their direction. She was pretty. Blond hair. Elegant. The man had his back to me but I could see his hair was black as night and his shoulders broad and strong. There was a stillness about him, an economy of movement that told me he could handle himself. I spent my day training with men strong enough to lift a small car with one hand, so there was no reason to give him even a second look but there was something about those shoulders, the way he held himself, that caught my attention. *Something familiar.*

My heart bumped my ribs and I felt a moment of sick panic and then I noticed half the women in the room were also looking at him.

I forced myself to breathe. He was a smoking-hot guy, that was all. Even from the back, he looked insanely good. Who wouldn't look?

It wasn't anyone I knew. Just some random stranger who had happened to pick the same restaurant as us.

'Rosie?' Brian sounded irritated that he'd lost my attention and I tried to forget about Muscle Man seated to my right. I didn't need a hot guy in my life. I had enough trouble with the lukewarm variety.

'Relax. I don't want to hurt you, Brian.' I was lying. Right at that moment I wanted to. Wondering what I'd ever seen in him, I sat back in my chair and tried to visualize fluffy kittens and other gentle soothing images to calm myself. 'We're supposed to be dating. Why would I want to hurt you?'

'I'm not saying that you do. Just that you *could*. And that feels a little weird, if I'm honest. A man likes to feel like a man, you know? And that thing you do…'

'That *thing?* Are you talking about Muay Thai or karate?' I noticed that the man at the next table sat a little straighter. I had a feeling he was listening to my conversation.

'Both! Whatever it's called, it's scary. I don't mind that you work as an instructor and a personal trainer—'

'Thanks.'

Detecting sarcasm, he sent me a swift frown. 'It's the fight-ing that's embarrassing.'

'You mean sparring? Competitions? Why is it embarrass-ing?'

'Let's say, for the sake of argument, we carry on seeing each other. Eventually I'm going to want to introduce you to my mother. What would I say? This is Rosie Miller—just ig-nore the fact that she's limping. She has the best scissor kick on the circuit.'

'I'm proud of my scissor kick. I work hard on my scissor kick.'

'For the record, the last girl I dated liked baking and book club.'

Baking and book club?

I stared at him, wondering whether to kill him now or wait until after dessert.

It was chocolate brownie, my favourite, so I decided to wait. I wasn't hungry, but no woman ate chocolate because she was hungry.

'Given that you're breaking up with me, let me give you some feedback here.' I leaned forward and pushed my arms against my sides to gain his attention—it was the only way I could produce any cleavage. 'Firstly, I am not interested in any relationship that culminates in meeting a guy's mother. Secondly, your manhood should not be threatened by who you date.'

'That's easy for you to say.' His desperation was coloured by a hint of sulk. 'We both know that if we were attacked, you'd be the one defending me, not the other way round. How is that supposed to make me feel?'

'Er…relieved?' I heard the man at the next table cough and I turned my head sharply but he was leaning toward his companion, attentive. I wondered if he was telling her she should join a book group.

'It makes me feel humiliated!' Brian hissed. 'All I'm saying is that it would be nice if you at least pretended to be a little vulnerable. Once in a while you could act like a girl.'

It was the lowest of blows.

He was telling me I wasn't feminine.

I felt the sting of tears behind my eyes and blinked furiously.

Why did I even care? It wasn't as if I thought Brian was my happily-ever-after. But happy to the end of dessert would have been nice.

And I had no intention of changing who I was to make him happy. My mother had done that and it had led to misery for all of us. I was determined to find someone who liked me the way I was.

Could the evening get any worse?

I sat there trying to catch my breath and then the man at the table finally turned his head and my evening was suddenly a whole lot worse, because it wasn't some stranger who sat there. It wasn't some nameless, faceless hot guy who a woman could fantasize about but never see again.

It was Hunter Black. Hunter, the first guy I'd ever dated. The first guy I'd slept with. The man who had taught me that a broken heart was more painful than a broken bone.

My nemesis.

His dark gaze burned into mine and suddenly I couldn't breathe.

Shit, *shit*.

I'd really believed I wouldn't feel anything if I saw him again. I'd told myself that if he ever reappeared in my life, I probably wouldn't even notice him. I'd walk right past, thinking he looked like someone I used to know.

I hadn't expected this gut-wrenching reaction. I felt as if I'd been hit by a truck and left in the gutter like roadkill.

Looking away, I stood up, scrabbled for my purse and knocked over my wine.

Brian cursed and tried to save his jacket and tie from the flood. 'Rosie, what are you doing?'

I was running. Running like hell. 'You're breaking up with me. I don't see the point in hanging around to watch the whole movie when I already know the ending.' I opened my purse and dropped a couple of notes on the table and, yes, a lot of other crap, too—I was probably the first person to try and pay a bill in old train tickets. 'As I threaten your manhood, I'll assume you don't want me to walk you home.'

Exercising supreme dignity and awesome balance, I strode out of the restaurant as fast as I could on those heels. My legs turned to liquid—not vodka, sadly—my heart was hammering and my palms were clammy.

*Don't let him follow me. Please don't let him follow me.*

And I wasn't talking about Brian.

I kept telling myself Hunter was with a woman, that he wouldn't just walk out on her, but that logic didn't reassure me.

How could it, when he'd once walked out on me?

Hunter did what suited him. If he wanted to walk, he'd walk. And if he wanted to follow me, he'd follow me.

I couldn't calm the feeling of panic or the wild need to put as much distance between myself and him as possible.

I heard voices behind me and I was so desperate to get away I almost stepped into the road.

A horn blared.

I looked frantically over my shoulder and saw the group of men who had been drinking at the bar appear at the door of the restaurant. Apart from wondering why they'd left when they'd appeared to be having a good time, I barely spared them a glance. I was too busy looking for Hunter, still terrified that he was going to follow me, although why I thought that, I had no idea. I hadn't seen him for five years and he'd not sent me as much as a text, so he was hardly likely to be rushing to exchange news and phone numbers.

Relieved there was no sign of him, I dived down the alleyway that ran down the side of the bar and connected with the main road. Far ahead I could see lights as cars whizzed past, but here in the narrow street it was dark and quiet.

I walked quickly, heart pounding. What was he doing here? Was he back in London permanently? Did he live close by?

The questions ran through my head and all I could think about was getting out of there.

Hayley was at home. We'd open a bottle of wine and watch the latest episode of *Girls*.

Scrunched-up newspaper brushed against my ankles and I picked my way through the mess, wondering why people had to be so gross in their habits. A cat crossed my path, eyes glinting in the darkness, and I was trying to remember if that was lucky or unlucky when I heard footsteps behind me.

They came at me without warning. Surrounded me.

And I knew, cat or no cat, my luck had run out.

# 2

I TURNED, THINKING it was a good job my hobbies didn't include baking or book group, because these guys didn't look as if they wanted a cupcake or my tip for a good bedtime read.

There were four of them, the men from the bar, and only now did I realize that walking down this alley had been a mistake. I'd been intent on getting away from Hunter. I hadn't thought about anything else. For the first time in as long as I could remember, I hadn't thought about my personal safety.

'Hey, pretty girl, looks like you walked out on your date.' The one who had smiled at me took the lead. 'Good decision. Want to go someplace and have some fun?'

'No.' I said it clearly so there could be no mistake. 'I'm going home. Alone.' I checked out my options swiftly. I was halfway down the street, so there was no obvious escape and there was no other person in sight.

I was on my own apart from the cat, but he'd walked away with a disdainful flick of his black tail. You can always rely on a cat to do his own thing in a crisis.

I taught people to be aware, to walk away from a fight, and here I was slap bang in the middle of a risky situation. In my haste to put distance between Hunter and me, I'd broken all my own rules.

The second man stepped in front of me. He was bigger, heavier than the first guy, probably a little out of condition but his bulk gave him advantage and I could see from the glitter in his eyes he'd been drinking.

I stepped back, still hoping to walk and talk my way out of the situation.

'Excuse me.'

'What's the rush? Don't you think that's a little unfriendly?'

'What I think,' I said clearly, 'is that you should go wherever you're going and leave me to go where I'm going. And those two places are not the same.'

'Maybe they are, kitten.' The smile held just a hint of nasty. He moved toward me, pressing me back against the wall, crowding me, caging me. I didn't hesitate. I lifted my knee, power driving through my hips as I kicked him. The transformation from kitten to tiger caught him by surprise. He doubled over and I spun and caught him with my elbow. Shock gave me the window I'd been hoping for to escape but sprinting was impossible in my heels and I'd barely made it a few steps when two of them yanked me back. My head smacked against the wall and pain exploded.

*Holy crap.*

I'd lost the element of surprise and I was about to scream when Hunter emerged out of the darkness. His face was barely visible, his bulk menacing in the shadows.

'Let her go.' He didn't raise his voice, but I felt the man's hold on me slacken.

The guy I'd kicked was rubbing his leg. 'Walk away. This is nothing to do with you.'

Hunter didn't move. That might have surprised them but it didn't surprise me. He never had been any good at following orders. He'd grown up in a part of London that most people avoided, so a dark street filled with litter and city types who couldn't hold their drink was unlikely to elevate his excitement levels.

'I told you to let her go.' He stood dangerously still, powerful legs braced apart. He was so damn sure of himself and my stomach curled and my limbs felt like overcooked spaghetti.

That confidence and assurance had been irresistible to an underconfident eighteen-year-old. To me he'd seemed like a cross between a god and a guardian angel. I'd wrapped my shaky, uncertain self around him like a plant desperate for support, using his strength instead of developing my own. When he'd walked away, I'd crumpled.

It embarrassed me to remember how pathetic I'd been. The memory was so humiliating I tried not to think about it. I tried not to think about *him*. Deep down I knew he'd done the right thing to break it off—although I didn't think he needed to have been quite so brutal in the execution. I'd been so clingy, so dependent, so good at leaning on him I'd forgotten how to stand upright by myself. Never had a girl been so crazily in love with a man as I'd been with Hunter.

And I should have known better. My sister and I had camped out on the battlefield of our parents' divorce, and believe me, it was a bloody experience. We'd both graduated from childhood totally screwed up about relationships.

When you witness a savage divorce, it can do one of two things to you. Either you decide marriage is something to be avoided at all costs, which is what my sister, Hayley, did, or you decide you're going to do it differently. That was what I did. I was never going to make the mistakes my parents made, because I was going to pick the right guy.

And then I'd met Hunter and I'd thought I'd fallen into the

fairy tale. Compared to him Prince Charming would have looked like a loser.

The man holding me let go of my wrist and stepped forward. 'There are four of us and one of you.'

Still Hunter didn't move. 'It's an uneven fight, which is why I'm telling you to walk away.'

I was the only one who understood his meaning. The four men thought the odds were in their favour.

I knew differently.

Mention Hunter's name in the world of martial arts, and everyone will know who you're talking about. His skill had been noticed at an early age and it was that skill that had won him championships and sent him across the globe to Japan and Thailand to study with the very best.

He had choreographed fight scenes for movies and appeared in a few. Not that I'd ever seen him on the big screen. I'd been trying to get him out of my head, so the last thing I needed was to be looking at a magnified version.

These four city types didn't look further than the suit.

They saw one man. They didn't see the power.

They came at him simultaneously and he unleashed that power in a series of controlled movements that had two guys bent over and groaning in pain within seconds and the other two retreating in shock. It shouldn't have surprised me. Hunter was respected, revered in some circles, as a strong, aggressive fighter and an inspirational instructor. But still, watching him in action made my stomach swoop.

I suddenly realized I was no longer being held.

'Get in the car!' His rough command penetrated my brain but I simply stared at him, frozen, because he was suggesting I go with him. For the first time in my life I understood the phrase 'between the devil and the deep blue sea.' And he wasn't the sea.

My teeth were chattering and I heard him curse softly. 'Rosie, get in the damn car. Move.'

I turned my head and saw the low black sports car parked at the side of the road with the door open. Was it really a step up to be trapped alone in a car with Hunter Black?

Without giving me more time to make the decision, he grabbed my hand and hauled me the short distance, all but bundled me inside and closed the door.

I breathed in the smell of expensive leather and elite super car.

Apart from thinking that Hollywood obviously paid well, I wasn't surprised.

Hunter had always been obsessed with power and speed. On my eighteenth birthday he'd given me a ride on the back of his motorcycle. I'd sat there, pressed against the power of the bike and the power of the man as we'd roared over London Bridge at two in the morning, realizing I'd never truly felt excitement before that moment. It was that night, right there wound around Hunter's hard, muscular frame, that I'd discovered the difference between living and being *alive*. That was the night our relationship had changed. Before that we'd had hidden places. Secrets. By the time we woke up in the morning there were no secrets left.

After that everything had been a lot like that bike ride. Wild, exhilarating and dangerous.

I'd loved the fact that he knew me. Really knew me.

He slid into the car next to me and the doors locked with a reassuring clunk.

I hadn't seen him since the day he'd walked out and now here we were, trapped together in this confined space. I was so aware of him I could hardly breathe. The scent, the power, *the man*. The air was thick with tension. I could have reached out and touched that strong, muscular thigh but instead I kept my hands clasped in my lap and my eyes straight ahead.

I'd assumed if I ever saw him again I wouldn't feel a thing.

I hated being wrong.

I felt as if I'd been plugged into an electric socket. The air hummed and crackled with unbearable tension. He was insanely attractive, of course, but I knew that wasn't what was happening here. It was something deeper. Something far more scary and uncontrollable.

I wondered if it was just me but then he turned his head at the same time I did and our eyes met. That brief exchange of glances was so intense I half expected to hear a crash of thunder.

His eyes were a dark velvet-black and the way he was looking at me told me he was feeling everything I was feeling. How could a single glance be so intimate?

My heart was pounding. I wanted to get out of the car so I could work out what all of this meant.

I wanted to get home.

I waited for him to ask me where I was living so he could drop me home, but he didn't. Instead he pulled away and joined the flow of traffic. He didn't say a word. No 'How have you been?' Or 'I'm sorry I left.'

Just tense, pulsing silence so heavy and oppressive it was like being covered in a thick blanket. And awareness. That throbbing, skin-tingling awareness that only ever happened when I was with this man.

The restaurant was close to Fit and Physical, where I worked, overlooking the river. Usually I loved London at night. I loved the lights, the reflection of buildings on the water, the trees, the crush of people and the general air of excitement that comes from living in the capital. Tonight I barely looked at the city that was my home.

I heard a throaty growl and for a moment I thought it was the car and then realized it was him.

'Why were you with him?' His jaw was clenched, his tone savage and I glanced across at him, stunned by the depth of emotion in his voice because Hunter was the most controlled person I'd ever met. He was the original Mr. Cool. Not tonight. He was simmering with fury and right on the edge of control. I realized that the reason he hadn't spoken was that he was angry.

'Who I'm with is none of your business.'

'Why would you choose to spend your evening with a guy who thinks you should be doing baking and book club?'

He'd heard that?

I'd thought embarrassment was a split dress at a wedding—ask my sister about that one—but I discovered this was far, *far* worse.

Let's be honest. When a girl finally meets up with the guy who broke her heart, she wants everything to be perfect. She wants perfect hair, a perfect body, a perfect life. Most of all she wants to be in the perfect relationship so that he can see what he gave up. She doesn't just want him to feel a sting of regret; she wants him contorted with it. She wants to smile and admit that breaking up with him was the best thing that ever happened because it put her on this path to lifestyle nirvana. The one thing she absolutely doesn't want, especially in my case, is for him to have to rescue her.

I wanted to crawl onto the floor of his car and curl up there unnoticed.

I wanted to rewind time and spend the evening in a deep bubble bath with the latest issue of *Cosmo*. Most of all I didn't want to feel this way. The truth was I dated men like Brian because I didn't want to feel as if I'd been singed by wildfire.

'You can drop me here and get back to your date. I'll take the underground.'

'Because walking down a dark alleyway alone at night wasn't enough of a bad decision?'

He'd always been protective. He'd always tried to keep me from being hurt. The irony was that in the end he'd been the one who had hurt me.

'I travel on the underground all the time.'

'Not when you're with me.'

Heat flooded through me. 'I'm not with you.'

'Right now you are.' His tone was savage. 'And unlike your useless date, I'm not leaving you.'

'Why? Have you suddenly developed a conscience?' I watched as two streaks of colour highlighted his cheekbones and knew I'd scored a point. 'Look, I've never been one for reunions, so just stop the damn car and—'

'What the hell were you doing going out with a guy like him in the first place? He's not the right man for you.'

'You don't know anything about me.'

'I know everything about you.' His husky tone was deeply personal and I felt everything tighten inside me.

The chemistry between us had always been explosive.

I'd assumed it was because he was my first, but I was fast realizing his ranking had nothing to do with it.

I stole a glance at his profile, wondering what it was about him that made me feel this way. He had the same features as anyone else: eyes, mouth, nose—his nose had been broken a couple of times. But something about the way those features had been assembled on him just worked. He looked tough, like someone who could handle himself—probably because he could—and the combination of rugged good looks and a hard body was pretty irresistible.

I felt a pang of regret that I'd wasted the time I'd had with him. Instead of just enjoying myself and having fun, which was what I should have done at eighteen, I'd been clingy and needy. Part of me wished I'd met him a few years later. Then we would have set the world alight.

But it was too late for all of that.

'Just drop me off and go back to the blonde.'

'You don't need to be jealous. She's a colleague.'

'I'm not jealous.' But I was, and I hated that. I hated the fact that he made me feel that way after all this time. 'Fuck you, Hunter.'

And I had, of course. If there was one thing we'd been good at, it was sex.

His knuckles were white on the wheel.

His head turned briefly and his gaze met mine again.

It was like the collision of two tectonic plates. I felt the tremor right through me from the top of my scalp to the soles of my feet and for a moment I was back there in the madness of it, my mind twisted by the ferocious sexual chemistry that only happened when we were together.

With a soft curse, he dragged his gaze from mine and shifted gears in a savage movement that made me flinch. 'You saw those guys looking at you and yet you just walked out and let them follow you.'

'I'm not responsible for their bad behaviour. A woman should be free to walk where she likes without fear of being accosted by losers.'

'You put yourself in a position where those losers could have hurt you.'

'So you're saying it's my fault they behaved badly?'

He clenched his jaw. 'No, I'm not saying that.'

I kept my hands clasped in my lap because the craving to touch him was scarily strong. 'I didn't know they were behind me. I wasn't paying attention. I was upset.'

'Because that guy told you to learn to bake cakes?'

No, because I'd seen *him*. All I'd wanted to do was run.

I was a coward. I prided myself on being gutsy and strong and I'd fled like a rabbit being chased by a fox.

'I didn't see any point in prolonging the evening. I've had a long week.'

'Did you run because of me?'

'Oh, please....' Now I was doing a Brian, leaving my sentences unfinished, but in my case it was because I didn't want to tell the truth and I was a hopeless liar.

Hunter didn't bother inserting the words I hadn't spoken. He didn't have to. He already knew the answer to that one. He'd always been able to read me. We probably could have had an entire conversation without opening our mouths.

Keeping his eyes fixed on the road, he drove past the Houses of Parliament up to Buckingham Palace and then drove through Hyde Park, headlights bouncing off trees and sending a shimmer of light across the Serpentine pond. I didn't own a car. For a start, I didn't have the money to run one, but in London there was no point. Why spend the whole day sitting in traffic?

Hunter reached into a pocket in the car and handed me a dressing pad. 'Your head is bleeding.'

'It's nothing.' A bit of blood was the least of my worries. I had bigger concerns, like the fact my heart was hammering. It didn't feel normal to me. 'I had the situation under control. You didn't need to help out.' I took the pad, ripped it open and pushed it against my forehead, wondering what else he carried in this car. I hoped he had a defibrillator, because I was pretty sure I was going to need one.

'If I hadn't arrived when I did, you'd be a crime statistic.'

'I was doing just fine.'

'Your balance was wrong. You need to watch the way you

drive your leg. You're straightening too soon and losing power. You need a ninety-degree angle. You need to bend more. And turn your hips.'

I was trying not to think about my hips. I was trying not to think about any part of my body, especially not the parts that were near my pelvis. I was worried I was about to catch fire.

For a moment I wondered if I was the only one feeling this way and then I saw his knuckles, white on the wheel, and realized he was struggling, too.

'Why did you follow me?'

'Because I knew you were upset. I wasn't going to leave you alone in that situation.'

'Why? You left me without a backward glance five years ago, so it's a little late to develop a protective streak.' I thought it was hypocritical of him to pretend he cared about my well-being when he'd once left me in a million pieces bleeding. Maybe that's a little dramatic, but that's how it felt.

His shoulders tensed and I realised that, far from seeming indifferent, I'd just revealed a wound the size of a continent.

# 3

OH, CRAP.

The first thing our mother taught us was never to show a man you're broken-hearted. I'd virtually dropped the pieces of mine in his lap.

'What I mean is, I've learned to look after myself.' I realized we were in Notting Hill and felt unnerved. 'How do you know where I live?'

'There are some things we need to talk about, but first I want to check that head of yours.'

I wanted to check my head, too. What had possessed me to climb into a car with Hunter Black? Obviously I had a concussion. I needed a health check, or at the very least a reality check.

'We don't have anything to talk about, but I do want to know how you have my address.'

He didn't answer me. Instead he took a right and then a left into the leafy, tree-lined street where I lived with my sister.

Our apartment was on the top floor of a lovely brick building, with views over the rooftops toward Kensington Gardens. If you stood on tiptoe and stuck your head out of our bathroom window, you could see Prince Harry (only kidding, sadly). We were right in the middle of shops, restaurants and the market. I loved it. Of course, since Hayley and Nico got together—you probably felt the ground shake—I'd had it to myself quite a bit. I didn't mind that. It meant I could practise in the living room without accidently kicking her or getting yelled at when I knocked a lamp off the table. Normally coming home soothed me. Tonight I was officially freaked out.

'Good night, Hunter. Thanks for the lift.'

'Is Hayley home?'

'How do I know? And why do you care?'

'You had a blow to the head. I'm not leaving you alone.'

'I want you to leave me alone.' I was fumbling with my seat belt, fingers slippery and shaky with nerves. Turned out I couldn't even do that without help and I felt the warm strength of his hand as it covered mine.

His fingers were warm, strong and totally steady and it irritated me that he had so much control when I had none.

He leaned forward and his jaw, dark with stubble, was only inches from my eyes. I looked at the sensual curve of his lips and the urge to press my mouth against his was almost painful.

And then he looked at me and I knew he was fighting the same urge.

For a moment we sat there, the moment of intimacy disturbed by the flash of headlights from a passing car.

Mouth tight, he unclipped my seat belt. 'You're bleeding. I should have taken you to the E.R.'

'It's nothing.' I was struggling to focus, but it had nothing to do with the blow to my head. There was something about being close to Hunter Black that made the most level-headed of women dizzy. 'I'll be fine. Good night. Great to catch up with you again after all this time. Have a nice life.'

I never was any good at delivering sarcasm, a fact confirmed by his smile. It was a slow, sexy, slightly exasperated smile that acknowledged everything that lay between us. I didn't want to acknowledge it. I preferred to step over it with my eyes shut.

Desperate to get away from that smile, those shoulders, *the man,* I virtually scrambled out of his car and sprinted to the door.

'Stairs or elevator?' He was right behind me and I gritted my teeth. When I was eighteen, he'd left me at acceleration speeds that would have left his car standing, but now I couldn't shake him off.

'You've spent too long in Hollywood. We say *lift.* And you can go now.'

'Not before I've seen you safely home.'

'I'm home.' I didn't feel up to the stairs—not that I would have admitted that in a million years—so I stepped into the tiny lift but the moment he stepped in after me I realized my mistake. We were on the second floor. To be honest, it was crazy that we even had a lift in this building. The space was barely big enough for two people. It certainly wasn't big enough for two people who were trying to keep their distance. My arm brushed against his and I flattened myself against the doors.

It was only two floors but it felt like going to the top of the Empire State Building. Every one of those floors felt like twenty. Every second felt like an hour. I could feel his gaze on me and it took all my willpower not to look at him.

I was determined not to.

I wasn't going to.

I wasn't…

*Crap.*

I turned my head.

My eyes moved to his chest, to the narrow strip of his tie, the silk of his shirt and upward to the dark depths of his eyes.

I hated him for walking away so easily, for not finding me impossible to leave—and I hated myself for caring so much—but that didn't change the fact he was spectacular. His features were intensely masculine, his hair black as the devil, cropped too short to soften those hard features. No one would argue that Hunter's hotness factor was right up in quadruple figures. And I didn't need to wonder what it would be like to be kissed by him. I knew. The memory was embedded deep in my brain. I hadn't been able to delete it.

I told myself it was the bang on my head that was making me feel swimmy. Anything other than admit it was him.

I hated him for making me want him again.

'It's good to see you again, Ninja.' The combination of his tone and the way he was looking at me made me feel as if someone had kicked my legs out from under me.

'I don't feel the same way. And don't call me Ninja.'

It made me think of the day we'd first spoken. I was sixteen and I'd lost a competition to a girl from a rival karate club. I'd been furious with myself, not least because I should have won. I would have, but I hadn't been concentrating. Instead I'd been glancing around the room to see if my parents were going to show up and embarrass me. They went through a hideous phase where they both showed up to everything, not because they cared but because they were trying to outdo each other in proving who was the better parent. In the end neither of them came. I probably should have been relieved they hadn't been there to witness my humiliation, but I wasn't. It just proved what I already knew. That neither of them cared.

I sat at the edge of the gym on my own, putting more energy into holding back tears than I'd ever put into beating my opponent, when Hunter squatted down in front of me.

I knew who he was. Who didn't? All the girls were crazy about Hunter. He was twenty years old, a skilled fighter, the youngest black belt our club had ever had and seriously hot, but he was too focused on training to be interested in a relationship, and anyway, he wouldn't have noticed me, because I was too young. Right at that moment I would have fast-forwarded time if that had been an option.

'Are you all right?'

I looked at him. 'I lost. I made mistakes.'

'That's the past. Next time you'll win, Rosie.'

For some reason the fact that he knew my name made me feel better.

'It doesn't matter anyway,' I muttered. 'No one will be watching.'

'I'll be watching.' He held out his hand and pulled me to my feet. 'Now go back out there, forget what's in the past and start fresh. Watch your balance. Keep your focus and concentration. Mistakes are learning experiences. Move on. Forget everything else in your life. That's what I do.'

I looked up at him, skinny, angular teenage me, and tried to imagine this broad-shouldered god having anything in his life he needed to forget. 'You have stuff you need to forget?'

He gave a faint smile and brushed a stray tear away from my face with the pad of his thumb. 'Everyone does, Ninja.'

Ninja.

I liked the name. It made me feel strong and suddenly I didn't feel like crying anymore.

He might have said something else but at that moment my sister flew across the room, school bag heavy with books banging against her hip. Her hair had half escaped from her ponytail and her breasts were doing their best to push the buttons of her shirt right out of the holes.

'Sorry I'm late. I had extra maths tuition and then Mum and Dad were arguing about where we were going to spend Christmas, so I gave up and left them. I ran all the way.'

My parents hadn't made it but my sister was here.

Hunter smiled at me and let his hand drop. 'Now you have two people watching you.'

I fell in love with him right there and then. Not because he was hot but because he cared.

There were a hundred other things he could have been doing, girls he could have been smiling at or flirting with, but he'd chosen to spend his time watching gawky, awkward, messed-up sixteen-year-old me in her karate competition.

From that moment on I no longer minded whether my parents turned up or not. I had Hunter. He was the one certain thing in my very uncertain world. He watched every competition; he offered advice; he trained with me. I knew he wasn't interested in me *like that*. I was just a kid. But suddenly I wasn't a kid anymore and on my eighteenth birthday he stopped treating me as one.

Everything changed that night, apart from the fact he still called me Ninja.

It was my nickname and it made me feel warm and special.

Hearing him saying it now was like having a knife twisted in my insides because it reminded me so much of that horrible messed-up time.

I felt the breath moving in and out of my lungs and I was holding myself still so there was no chance I'd accidently brush against him a second time. I could feel the heat in my cheeks and I stared at the wall even though I could feel him watching, cool and calm.

I stumbled out of the lift in my haste to get away from him, took the few stairs that led to our attic flat and had my keys in my hand when the door opened.

Hayley stood there. She was wearing skin-tight jeans and a top that emphasized the fact she'd inherited the breast DNA. The fact that her hair was loose and messy told me that Nico had been round. 'How was boring Brian?' Her voice trailed off as she saw my forehead. 'Oh my *God,* what happened? Only you can come back from a dinner date with a black eye.'

'It's not a black eye.'

'Did it happen at work? You need another job. Or at least a different hobby. I recommend astronomy.' And then she saw Hunter. She couldn't have looked more surprised if Mars had bashed into Pluto. Her eyes went wide and then flew to mine.

I couldn't exactly blame her for looking confused.

For the past five years I'd refused to talk about Hunter. He was a subject we avoided. And suddenly here he was, dominating our doorstep.

I could tell she didn't have a clue what she was supposed to say.

She just didn't get it and I didn't blame her.

She sent me a look that said 'WTF.'

I sent her a silent transmission. *Play it cool.*

'I'm hallucinating,' she muttered. 'For a moment I thought I saw a rat on my doorstep.'

'Hayley.' Unmoved by the less than effusive welcome, Hunter placed his hand on my lower back and urged me into the apartment.

'She needs to sit down.'

I heard my sister mutter, 'She's not the only one,' and suddenly felt a flood of relief that she was here and I was no longer on my own with this. I'd heard people say how much they loved being an only child, how great it was to have all that attention. I'd never understood that. I couldn't imagine what my life would look like if it didn't have my sister in it. I was pretty sure it would be awful. I'd probably pretend it was great, because that's what people did, wasn't it? There were some things you were stuck with and some things you'd never admit to not liking.

Being stuck with my sister was the best thing that had ever happened to me (apart from the fact she ended up with the whole breast gene. I found that hard to forgive).

'What are you doing here, Hunter?' Hayley sounded so fierce I jumped, but Hunter didn't react.

'Bringing Rosie home. I need ice and dressing pads for her head.'

'I can sort out my own head.' Actually I couldn't. If I could have sorted out my own head, I would have done it long ago and I wouldn't have been so screwed up about him. When it came to Hunter, my brain was as tangled as the cord of my headphones.

'What happened to her head?' Hayley sounded furious. 'If you've hurt her again, Hunter Black, I swear I will donate your body to medical science.'

'That happens when you're dead. I'm still alive.'

My sister sent him a dark look. 'I could fix that.' She had her arm round me and was drawing me toward the sofa. 'Don't get blood on it. You know I'm a rubbish housekeeper and I'm still dealing with the coffee stain from last month.' My sister's idea of dealing with a coffee stain was simply to turn the sofa cushion over.

But I could tell she was worried and she paused for a moment, torn between the need to stop my head bleeding and a reluctance to leave me alone with Hunter.

Hunter didn't wait to be shown around our apartment. He found the kitchen, grabbed ice packs out of the fridge, wrapped them in a towel and brought them back to where I was sitting.

He was a good person to have around in a crisis. The problem was that in my case he was usually the one causing the crisis.

My sister tapped her foot. 'You should go now, Hunter.'

'I'm not leaving until I know she's all right.'

'Of course she's all right,' my sister snapped. 'She's with me. Who do you think looked after her when you walked out? I did. And you didn't exactly hang around to check on her, did you? So you can stop pretending to be caring. You left her in pieces.'

So much for my dignity. 'Hayley—'

'She cried every night for six months! She didn't eat. She lost weight. So don't think she's going to agree to start that whole thing with you up again just because you happen to have shown up in her life again.'

Holy crap. *'Hayley!'*

'She pretends she's over you—'

'I *am* over him!'

'—but she hasn't been serious about a man since.' My sister was in full flow, raging forward like a river that had burst its banks. 'She dates men she can never, ever fall in love with, which basically means she has a boring sex life, and no girl of her age deserves a boring sex life, especially when she's in her sexual prime! Do you know what I bought her for her birthday last year? A vibrator! And batteries are fucking expensive! And it's your fault.'

Hunter blinked. 'It's my fault batteries are expensive?'

'It's your fault she gets through so many. You are responsible for that, Hunter Black. You and no one else.'

I was going to kill her. I would have liked to do it slowly but as I was about to die of humiliation, there was no time to waste. I glared at her, hoping she'd take the hint and shut up but it was too late—Hayley was in full protective-sister mode, firing on all cylinders like one of the rockets that fascinated her so much, and Hunter was looking at me with that smouldering, intense gaze that stripped me bare.

He was one of the few people, possibly the only person apart from Hayley, who had ever understood me. There was a time when that had turned me on. Now it was just a great big fat inconvenience. I didn't want him in my head, poking around in my deepest, darkest secrets. It made me feel vulnerable.

I wasn't that girl anymore. I'd grown up. Sure, I had a few scars, but who didn't?

As he'd once said to me, everyone had something.

'You should leave now,' I said stiffly. 'Thanks for the lift.'

He didn't budge. He stood there, those powerful legs spread, towering over us like a conquering warrior. 'Before I leave, I need to talk to you. There is something I need to say.'

Hayley pursed her lips. 'If it's sorry, then you're about five years too late.'

I was starting to wish my sister would turn into one of those people who never finished their sentences.

'There is nothing you need to say, Hunter. You were the one who told me to treat mistakes as learning experiences.' I closed my eyes because looking at him made my head hurt and my heart hurt. 'I learned. It's all fine.'

'It's not fine and you should definitely leave.' Hayley repeated my words like some sort of recording device. 'We know you're good at that because you've done it before.'

He stood there like Apollo, or maybe it was Zeus—sorry, Greek gods aren't my thing—his eyes on my face as if he was working something out.

Then his mouth tightened. 'All right. We'll do this another time.'

Another time? Over my dead body. This one time had been more than I could handle.

I was fast coming to the conclusion that reunions weren't for me.

As he strode out of our apartment, I waited for the click of the door and then flopped back on the sofa, on top of the magazine Hayley had been reading and the stuffed llama I'd bought her for Christmas.

Hayley flopped back with me. 'Holy crap.'

'Yes.' The llama was digging in my back and I pulled it out and flung it across the living room. 'What the hell were you thinking, telling him I was broken-hearted?'

'I'm sorry! I went into shock when I saw him standing there. My mouth and my brain lost the connection.'

'I know the feeling. Do we still have that fire blanket in the kitchen? I might need you to throw it over me to put out the flames.'

'He is hot, that's for sure.'

'I was talking about the flames of my embarrassment.'

'Oh.'

'What were you thinking, saying all those things?'

'I don't know! I wasn't expecting to see him. You could have warned me! You should have texted me or something. I had no idea Hunter was even back in London.'

'Neither did I until an hour ago.'

My sister thought about that. 'He is *smoking* hot.'

'He is not smoking hot.'

'Yeah, that's right, he's the scrawniest, most pathetic specimen of manhood that ever stepped over our threshold. It's amazing a gust of wind hasn't blown him over. Are you seriously trying to pretend you don't still want to rip his clothes off?'

'If I'd met him for the first time this evening, maybe. But we have history. It's all too complicated.'

'Only if you let it be. What did he mean when he said "We'll do this another time"?'

I pressed the ice pack against my head. 'Don't know, because I am never going to see him again.'

'But if you do?'

'I'll ignore him.'

She stuck her feet up on the arm of the sofa. 'He's even hotter than he used to be and that's saying something.'

'I don't need to hear that.'

'And you look great in that dress. He didn't take his eyes off you. The two of you have insane chemistry.'

'I don't need to hear that either.' Every time I thought about my embarrassing behaviour, I wanted to slide under the sofa—except you never quite knew what you were going to find under our sofa. 'I feel hot all over.'

My sister stood up. 'I'll get you that fire blanket.'

# 4

DESPITE MY THROBBING head, I showed up to work early. I wasn't going to let an unexpected encounter with Hunter derail my life. He was my past, not my future. We had new management. We were now officially owned by the Black Belt Corporation. There was no way I'd risk giving them any reason to get rid of me. Hopefully, they'd see my bruised head and take it as a sign I was dedicated to my job.

My first class was waiting. As well as karate, I taught self-defence and I'd had the same group of women for the past year. We talked about threat awareness—I felt as if I ought to sit in on my own class after what had happened the night before—and I went through the areas of the body most suscep-tible to attack, in my case my heart, and demonstrated basic self-defence techniques. Sometimes I thought these women turned up only for the companionship, but I enjoyed the class and I liked to think if they ever needed to defend themselves, they might remember what I'd taught them.

Today as I got them into position for the warm-up, all they could talk about was some hot guy they'd seen on the way into the gym. This wasn't unusual, because the place was teeming with hot guys. As day jobs went, it was a good one, which was another reason I was wary about the change of management.

'Have you seen him, Rosie?'

'Who?' I tried to get them to focus but it was hopeless. The whole hour passed like that, with them exchanging giggles and asides. At the end of the class I sent them all off for a cold shower.

I had an hour before I taught my under-sixteen karate class, and as the new manager still hadn't asked to see me, I decided to use the time to train. After the night before, I needed to let off steam.

I started with cardio. All martial arts place a heavy focus on body conditioning. It's not enough to practice competitive fighting techniques. You have to be fit. Sometimes I run in the morning before work. More often I just find time in my day to use one of the gym or fitness suites. I skip a lot. And although it makes people like Brian shudder, the truth is the Muay Thai is a very effective workout.

Huge glass walls looked over the river in our main gym, so at least you had a decent view while you were punishing your body.

The place was half-empty and I warmed up and then focused on bag work. Because we used hands, feet, knees and elbows to attack, the bags were longer and heavier than normal punch bags. Muay Thai was called *the art of eight limbs* for a reason. Kicking, kneeing and elbowing a kick bag increased your stamina and power. After the fiasco of the night before, I worked on driving the leg in repeat kicks. If I hadn't messed up, I wouldn't have needed to be rescued. I was going to make sure it didn't happen again. But as I smacked my shin into the bag, I didn't pretend it was one of those four guys; I pretended it was Hunter. I was almost enjoying myself until I heard his voice behind me.

'You're straightening your leg and losing power.'

For a moment I thought I'd imagined it because I was pretending to kick him.

No such luck.

Hunter was standing there, black T-shirt and track pants skimming a body hard with muscle. There was just a hint of the dangerous about him and a self-confidence that had always drawn me as much as his looks. Sexy didn't begin to describe him. My gaze locked on to his, blue on to black. I was out of breath from smacking my shin into the heavy bag and staring at him didn't do anything to calm my heart rate. 'What are you doing here? Are you stalking me?'

'How are you feeling?' He was looking at my head. 'Any aftereffects? Dizziness? Nausea?'

I had both those things but neither had anything to do with the blow to the head. Being in the same room as him turned my brain and my knees to pulp. 'I'm fine.'

He lifted his hand and pushed my hair aside so that he could take a better look. The warmth of his fingers brushed my skin and I felt as if I'd been electrocuted.

'What are you doing here?'

'I should be the one asking you that question. You should have taken the day off.'

'We've had a change of management. The last thing I need is to lose my job on top of everything else.'

'You wouldn't lose your job.'

'How do you know?'

His gaze slid back to mine. 'Because I'm the management.'

For a moment I thought I'd misheard and then I stared into those dark velvet eyes and knew I hadn't. 'Fit and Physical has been taken over by the Black Belt Corporation.'

'That's right. I own the Black Belt Corporation.'

'You?' It hadn't occurred to me it could be him. I felt stupid.

I hadn't taken any notice of the word *Black* in the company name. But now I thought about it, it was obvious. Hunter had trained in this place. Spent every day here growing up. He'd loved it as much as I did.

And he was back.

Now I really did feel sick.

'You own Fit and Physical?' My palms were sweaty. I wiped them over my workout pants. I noticed he was wearing the same black T-shirt all the staff wore and wondered why I hadn't seen that the moment he walked in.

'I was going to tell you last night but I thought you'd had enough of a shock for one evening.'

James, one of the other instructors, walked into the room. 'Mr. Black—er, Hunter, could I just—?'

'Not now.' Hunter didn't even turn his head. He kept his gaze fixed on me and my skin burned as if I'd lain naked in the heat of the midday sun. My mouth was as dry as if I'd hiked through the desert. Once again I wished I'd saved this man for a time when I was better able to cope with him. I'd wasted what could have been the hottest, most exciting relationship of my life on my messed-up teenage self. I wished I could wind the clock back. I'd ignore the angst and enjoy the man.

James took one look at Hunter's face and then mine and backed out of the room, no doubt to spread the word that Rosie Miller was about to get her marching orders from the new boss.

I stooped and picked up my water. 'Right. Well, I'd better leave.'

'Why would you leave?'

Because I was about to leap on him, strip him naked and enjoy the sex without any of the angst that went with relationships. 'I think it's best.'

'Are you really going to walk out on a job you enjoy because we were once lovers?'

We both knew he hadn't been just my lover—he'd been my everything. Hunter had filled all those empty gaps in my life and when he'd walked away, I hadn't been sure I'd hold together. It had been like playing emotional Jenga. Once that all-important piece had been removed, the whole structure had collapsed. It made me cringe to think about it.

Fortunately, I'd rebuilt myself and I was pretty robust now. I wasn't going to blow over in a strong wind and I wasn't going to let the threads of my life unravel over a man.

There was no way I would walk out on a job I loved just because working alongside Hunter reminded me of the most humiliating time of my life.

'I wasn't suggesting I leave the job,' I lied, 'simply the room. Unless you'd like me to leave the job?'

I dumped the problem right back in his lap.

Maybe he couldn't cope with working with me. Maybe he was afraid I'd revert to being that clingy, embarrassing creature he'd once known. I couldn't really blame him.

'You're exceptionally talented and I want talented people around me. That's the way to build a successful business. And we're going to grow this place into a successful business.'

The compliment robbed me of breath. So did his use of the word *we*.

I swallowed, wondering what it was about this man that turned me to a lump of quivering jelly. My skin tingled and my nerve endings hummed. I looked into his eyes and forgot where I was.

I was seconds away from doing something really stupid like kissing him when the door opened and another instructor put her head round. This time it was Caroline and the moment I saw the way she looked at Hunter, I realized he was the guy my self-defence class had been talking about.

Grateful for the interruption, I nodded and walked past him out of the room, trying to come to terms with the fact that my dream job had turned to torture. I was going to have to see him every day. Work with him. And not kiss him. I'd had my chance with him and I'd messed it up.

I taught the rest of my classes on automatic.

All I wanted to do was go home early, but I had a late one-to-one with a lovely guy who had lost four stone and was determined to lose another two. He never missed a session, so I wasn't going to be the one who let him down.

As usual, I was the last one in the building.

I walked into the female staff changing room and stripped off.

I stood under the water, letting it wash over me. All I could think of was Hunter. I adjusted the temperature to cold, wondering how I was going to work alongside him without revealing how I felt. I was going to have to take a lot of cold showers.

I pulled on yoga pants and a T-shirt, left my hair loose and walked out of the changing room slap into Hunter.

He put his hands on my shoulders to steady me and I felt the strength in those fingers and the heat of his body. Awareness shot through me. It was as if my body was programmed just to respond to him, which was frustrating on so many levels when you considered I was working hard to convince myself that this was going to be fine. That my self-control was up to this challenge.

'What are you doing here?' I blurted the words out and he raised an eyebrow.

'I own the place.'

'Thanks for reminding me. For a moment it had slipped my mind.'

His hands were still on my shoulders. 'We should talk, Ninja.'

'Not a good time. I've got to dash. I'm meeting Hayley.'

Instead of releasing me, he tightened his grip on my shoulders. 'Are you going to spend the whole time avoiding me?'

'I'm not avoiding you. But I have a life.' A pretty boring, mundane life that was depressingly low on hot men, but that was my own fault. 'Have a good evening, Hunter.' I tried to move away from him but we were still toe to toe.

'I have plans for this place. Exciting plans. Want to hear them?'

I had plans, too. They involved getting out of here as fast as possible. 'Er…maybe later.'

His eyes were hooded. 'You're finding this difficult.'

'Not at all, but I'm already late.' I peeled myself away from him and tried to walk away but I had shaky legs and tripped over my own feet, or maybe it was his feet. Either way, I landed against the solid wall of his chest.

*Oh, holy crap.*

I heard him curse softly. Felt his hands grip my arms. Felt heat, strength and pumping male power. He smelled delicious and I closed my eyes for a moment, breathing him in. I looked up and my eyes had a close-up view of his jaw with its five o'clock shadow. The contrast between us had always fascinated me. His dark to my light. I was strong, but my arms were lean and sinewy; his were bulky and powerful and his biceps felt as if someone had pushed rocks under his skin. Being this close to him made me dizzy. I was so aware of him. The chemistry was electric, as if my body refused to pay attention to the messages from my brain. There was a tightening low in my stomach, a growing heat that spread from my core to my limbs.

And then we were kissing.

Not tentatively. Not gently. It was rough and raw. Hot and

desperate. We kissed as if this were our last moment on Earth and we were going to suck it dry. His kiss was as skilled and every bit as exciting as I remembered. I felt the press of hard muscle through the fabric of his track pants, felt his hands cup my face as he focused all his attention on my mouth. It took one second for me to know for sure my teenage self hadn't exaggerated how this had felt. Two seconds to remember how it had been with this man. I was virtually crawling all over him in an attempt to get closer, but he held me firm and steady, his expert mouth drugging my brain, sending my head spinning in dizzy circles because Hunter didn't just take when he kissed—he gave.

I felt the thick ridge of his erection pressed against me, the hardness of his thighs, the solid strength of male muscle as he tightened his arms around me, kicked open the door to the changing room I'd just exited and propelled me back inside.

The door crashed back against the wall and I jumped. 'You'll be in trouble for destruction of property.'

'My property.' He growled the words against my mouth and I was wondering whether he was talking about me or the building when he flattened me against the wall and suddenly I couldn't think of anything but the way his mouth felt on mine.

My fingers were jammed in his hair. His hands were on my bottom, holding me hard against him. His mouth ravaged mine, hot and demanding. We were out of control. I knew it. He knew it. Neither of us did anything to stop it. Certainly not me. His hands slid inside my yoga pants. Heat flashed across my skin. I shifted restlessly against him, desperate for him to use those skilled fingers of his where I needed it most. He didn't. Instead he slowly drove me mad, stroking me with expert fingers, touching me with erotic precision until my hands dug hard into his scalp and I was begging against his mouth. I'd never been so desperate for anything. And then his fingers were sliding over me and inside me until finally I lost it. Pleasure exploded, hot pulsing pleasure, and I would have cried out but his mouth was on mine, smothering sound while his fingers felt every intimate moment of my release.

Somewhere in the distance a door slammed.

I heard him swear under his breath and the next moment he was hauling my yoga pants back up my shaking thighs and smoothing my tangled hair back from my face.

I didn't say anything. I didn't do anything. I just looked at him. And he looked at me.

He spoke first. 'I'm sorry.' His voice was thickened and his broad shoulders were rigid with tension. He was probably wondering what the hell he'd just done. I wondered if he was panicking in case I turned into that needy, clingy teenage version of myself. In fairness, that was the only version he'd ever known.

'Well—' my voice sounded husky '—that saves me buying batteries on my way home.' I managed what I hoped was a seductive smile. 'Thank you.'

Without giving him time to respond, I scooped up the bag I'd dropped and walked jauntily out of the changing rooms— which turned out to be a major challenge on shaking legs.

Only when I was safely out of the building and on the street did I allow myself to react.

I leaned against the wall for support and closed my eyes.

'You kissed him?' Hayley handed me a large glass of wine. 'You were going to ignore him and somehow ended up kissing him? How did that happen?'

'Turns out I have no willpower. And it was a bit more than kissing.'

My sister was sprawled on the floor surrounded by papers. She'd been working all day and a light glowed on her laptop.

It was Saturday night and for the first time in ages we weren't going out.

We'd ordered pizza and eaten it out of the box, slice by glorious slice, wearing our PJs, because if you couldn't be bothered to use plates, you certainly couldn't be bothered to get dressed.

'So how was it?' Hayley sipped her wine. 'Pretty boring and disappointing, right?' My silence must have answered her question, because she leaned across and filled my wineglass to the brim. 'You know your problem, don't you?'

'You don't need to list my problems. Brian already did that. It's a good job we broke up or my birthday gift from him would have been cake decorating classes.'

'Forget Brian. He didn't like the real you and every woman deserves a man who loves her the way she is.' She looked at me and I knew she was thinking about Mum. Dad had known exactly what he wanted in a woman. Mum wasn't it, but he'd married her anyway and tried to mould her into the person he wanted her to be. By the time he decided to upgrade, Mum was so misshapen she'd lost her real self under the fake version.

'We don't always get what we deserve,' I reminded Hayley darkly, and her cheeks dimpled into a wicked smile.

'I'm getting what I deserve. Several times a night.'

'Thanks. I really needed to hear that.'

But I was pleased for her because she didn't find this dating thing easy either.

Hayley was an engineer and men always found her job threatening. Apart from Nico. He was the first man she'd met who understood what she did. He found it cool that she knew her atoms from her assholes. In fact, they'd finally got it together at the wedding of the biggest asshole of them all—her ex.

'Sounds as if you just got what you deserved, too. You just need more of it. I'm planning your birthday, by the way.'

I felt a rush of warmth and love for my sister.

Hayley always organized my birthday parties. Not at the beginning, of course. To begin with we'd left it up to Mum and Dad because we'd been naive enough to think parties were their domain. That all changed on my ninth birthday. Some kids had entertainers—we had our parents. Dad hurled one of my presents at Mum (it was Cheerleader Barbie) and gave her a black eye. I think my friends thought they were watching a juggling act until Mum picked up the knife she'd put ready to cut my cake. After that it got a bit real.

From then on Hayley had taken over. Usually she talked a friend into holding it at their house so there was less chance of parental embarrassment. And most of our friends' parents felt so sorry for us they were happy to co-operate. We were 'those poor Miller sisters.' We were talked about in hushed voices with much pursing of lips and barely concealed sympathy. We were fed extra cakes and sugary treats as if an excess of chocolate frosting and blocked arteries might somehow compensate for the fact we were emotionally starved.

They felt sorry for us, but in some ways we felt lucky.

We had each other and we shared a bond none of our friends had with their siblings.

In fact, it was my parents who were responsible for me taking up karate. When they finally decided to part, they were determined to split everything evenly down the middle. Mum got the bed, so Dad took the sofa. She had the cat; he took the dog. It worked so neatly they decided to do the same with the kids. She was going to have Hayley and I was going with Dad. We didn't much care which parent we lived with but there was no way they were splitting us up. I won't bore you with the details but let's just say they didn't try that again.

But I'd taken up karate just in case.

I looked at my sister. My family. 'What I really want for my birthday is a decent sex life.'

'Oh no!' She pretended to look alarmed. 'That means I'll have to cancel those cake decorating classes I booked for you.'

'You're not funny.' But I was laughing because the idea of my sister booking me cake decorating classes was hilarious. Not that I'm a bad cook, but you won't find me twirling cute patterns on the tops of cupcakes.

She closed the pizza box. 'Think of all those lovely comforting carbs you'd bring home every week. And you wouldn't want to eat them, which would mean all the more for me.'

'And then I'd make you work them off in the gym. You were about to tell me what my problem is.' I executed a perfect roundhouse kick, which probably would have looked scary had I not been wearing my cute bunny pyjamas. I missed my sister's head by the width of a pizza crust but she'd lived with me for too long to bother ducking. 'What's my problem?'

'Apart from your congenital need to kick me in the head from time to time? Hunter was your first lover. You built him up into this godlike figure and you've compared every man to him ever since.'

'That's not true.'

'It is. The two of you were really close. When he walked away from you, he tore you in two and you never even had a chance to yell at him, because he was gone. It's hardly surprising you're still churned up inside. You have so much unfinished business. And you haven't allowed any of us to mention his name for the past five years. In your head he's still the perfect man.'

That got my attention. 'He is so *not* the perfect man. That isn't why I hate talking about him.'

'I know. You're embarrassed because you think you were

needy, but part of that was because you're romantic. You always were.'

I thought about what had just happened in the changing rooms.

I could have described it in many different ways, but the word *romantic* wouldn't have been anywhere in the description.

'You shouldn't feel bad about it.' My sister's voice was soft. 'Mum and Dad were behaving like idiots, but Hunter was always there. It's not surprising you latched on to him.'

'Please don't remind me.'

'That's all in the past. Answer me one question.' Hayley pushed the empty pizza box away with her foot. 'Who is the best sex you ever had?'

'My vibrator.' I said it flippantly but she carried on looking at me as only my sister can and I sighed. 'Hunter.'

'Right. You had amazing sex with him and you haven't had amazing sex since.'

I chewed my lip. I decided not to admit that tonight had been pretty amazing. 'And?'

'And you should have sex with him again. This time you've shaken off all the emotional baggage. It would be fun and you'd save a fortune on batteries.'

'No way. He's my boss.' Just thinking about working with him every day made me want to order another pizza. Ten inches—and yes, I'm still talking about the pizza—with extra cheese. And I'm not generally big on comfort eating. 'I wouldn't have sex with my boss.' Except that I already had, sort of.

*Crap.*

I wasn't sure I'd ever be able to use the changing rooms again.

Facing him on Monday was going to be a nightmare.

'I'm not doing this again. Not with Hunter.'

'Why not? You're not in love with him anymore. This time around, you can have the fun without any of the Romeo-and-Juliet drama. This time it's all on your terms. All the sex with none of the heartbreak.'

'I am not going to have sex with him.' I told myself what had happened in the changing room didn't count. 'No way.'

Hayley picked up the empty pizza box and stood up. 'Fine. Carry on dating guys like Brian, who isn't even strong enough to lift the cupcake he wants you to bake.'

'I don't judge guys by the size of their biceps.'

'Neither do I.'

'Just because you're having sex with an Italian stallion who has a brain *and* biceps, there is no need to be smug.'

'Do I look smug?' She smiled smugly. 'Take control. You're older. Wiser. You are working with a hot, sexy guy. It's a shame to waste him.'

'I'm not interested and neither is he.'

'You think not?' Her smile widened. 'For two people who aren't interested you generate a *lot* of electricity when you're in the same room. The two of you could solve the energy crisis with one touch.'

'I'm prepared to recycle and do my bit to conserve fossil fuels, but I'm not having sex with Hunter.'

# 5

I TRIED TO ignore him, really I did. I ignored him so hard I walked into walls while trying not to look at him.

I took my classes. I trained. I attended meetings and managed to look focused and professional, which was more than could be said of the rest of the female staff, who spent their time with their noses pressed to the glass windows of whichever space he happened to be working in.

Hunter managed focused and professional, too.

But that's the funny thing about intense sexual attraction. You can try and ignore it, but it's still there. You can feel it on your skin. It simmers in the air, wraps itself around you, seeps into your brain and makes concentration difficult. I knew without turning my head when he was in the room, and not just because I couldn't get any sense out of my female clients.

And he seemed to be avoiding me, too.

Neither of us mentioned what had happened in the changing room that night.

Our interaction was all business. At least, on the outside.

A week after he'd arrived to take control, he pulled us all into the meeting room on the top floor of the building and told us his plans for the business. He talked about his vision. Unfortunately, he did it while wearing a karate suit and everyone else's vision was focused on his broad, muscular chest rather than his presentation. I kept my eyes on the floor but it didn't help. I kept remembering how it had felt with his mouth on mine and his fingers deep inside me. That sort of intimacy isn't easy to forget.

I shifted in my chair and caught his eye.

*Shit.*

I was glad I wasn't the one giving the presentation. I would have been stammering and distracted but Hunter didn't falter.

With the benefit of five years apart and some distance, I could see now why I'd been overwhelmed by him. Dazzled. I didn't feel like quite so much of a fool for falling for him. He was impressive. Self-assured, confident, self-reliant. All the things I hadn't been as a teenager. He'd been around at a time of my life when I'd been at my most vulnerable. It was as if something in me had been looking to supplement what was missing, to borrow what I didn't have myself.

I'd been looking for security, consistency and dependability because I had none of those things at home. Using our parents as an example, Hayley chose to reject everything to do with marriage and settling with one person. She became a lone wolf. But I'd always been more of a pack person and Hunter was a born alpha.

I realized now that as well as friendship and sexual attraction, there had been a lot of other things mixed up in our relationship. I realized we hadn't really been equals.

Things were different now.

I'd built a life I loved, my sister was my family and we had a great bunch of friends. True, my sex life was mostly battery operated but a girl couldn't have everything.

'Are you joining us tonight? Team night out. We're going

to a club.' Caroline's mouth gleamed with freshly applied lip gloss. I turned away to avoid the glare, wondering if the extra shine was for Hunter's benefit.

'I don't think so.'

'Hunter wants us all there. He's really keen on team building. He wants us to bond.'

He and I had already done more than enough bonding.

I needed to keep my distance.

But Caroline was looking at me curiously and I realized that to not go would draw attention, so I nodded and decided to arrive late and leave early.

Like so many of my plans, that one backfired. Because I'd elected to arrive late, I found myself squashed in a booth, thigh to thigh with Hunter. He'd bought drinks, and everyone was laughing and enjoying themselves.

Everyone except me.

I couldn't think of anything but his thigh pressed against mine. I tried to ease away but James arrived, even later than me, and sat down on the other side of me, leaving me no choice but to move closer to Hunter.

My thigh was glued to his. I tried to ease it away but there was nowhere to go and I sat there keeping as still as I could, trying not to think about that night in the changing room. I stared at the dance floor and nursed my drink, wondering why on earth I'd agreed to come tonight.

Across from me Caroline stood up. 'Let's all dance.'

That sounded like a good idea but it turned out it wasn't. Dancing with Hunter, even in a group, did nothing to cool me down. I was so busy trying not to touch him I was barely moving. I was wearing my favourite red dress, which was actually little more than a stretchy tube. I loved it because it meant I could dance without fear of exposing myself, but tonight

I wasn't testing its capabilities. The floor was crowded and someone bumped into me, sending me slamming into him.

I felt his hands close over my arms, steadying me, and I shut my eyes. I decided right there and then that there was only so much torture a girl could take.

Muttering excuses, I plowed my way through the seething mass of gyrating bodies and out into the street. I crossed the road to the embankment and hung over the wall, looking at the river. Lights sparkled on the surface of the water. I wondered whether jumping in would cool me off.

'Are you all right?' His voice came from behind me and I breathed deeply, knowing I couldn't show him how I felt. Not this time.

'Just needed some air. Go back inside.'

But he didn't. Instead he stood next to me and stared at the river. 'I didn't know you worked for Fit and Physical until I took over the company and saw the staff list. I've made things difficult for you.'

'No, you haven't. It's no problem.'

'I enter a room, you leave it. When we're sitting next to each other, you stare straight ahead. We haven't talked about what happened.' His arm brushed against mine. He turned his head to look at me. 'I'm sorry.'

'Don't be.' I gave him my most sophisticated woman-of-the-world smile. 'You gave me a great start to the weekend. You're good. You always were.'

He didn't smile back. 'I'm not talking about the sex.'

'Oh.'

'You must hate me for what I did.'

Was that what he thought? I didn't know whether to laugh or be relieved he hadn't guessed the truth. If I hated anyone, it was myself.

'I don't hate you.'

A muscle flickered in his jaw. 'I walked out.'

'I don't blame you for doing it.'

'You didn't look pleased to see me the other night.'

'I was having a difficult evening. It was pretty frustrating that you just happened to show up when I was being dumped.'

'You shouldn't have been with him in the first place.' His voice was husky and sexy and I turned away to look across the water, hoping he couldn't see the burn in my cheeks.

'Look, what happened between us—that's the past. I don't blame you for any of it. I was a mess.' When he didn't respond, I turned my head and saw the shock in his eyes. 'What? Do you think I'm so lacking in self-insight I didn't know that? Hunter, I was terrible. Frankly, I don't know how you put up with me as long as you did. I was a nightmare. I can't even bear to think about it, because it embarrasses me so much.' Although it made me cringe to admit it, I actually felt better having said it. 'I'm the one who owes you an apology. I was like a piece of bindweed. I was a limpet and you were my rock.'

He breathed deeply and then lifted his hand and brushed his fingers over my cheek. 'You were adorable.'

No matter how hard I tried, I couldn't not respond to his touch. My stomach curled and knotted. 'I was needy, clingy and far too serious.'

He curved his hand round the nape of my neck, his thumb still on my cheek. 'I was afraid I couldn't live up to your expectations. I was afraid of letting you down. And I did.'

'We both know you did me a favour,' I muttered, 'even though your method was a bit brutal.' The most brutal thing had been accepting he hadn't loved me, but I wasn't going to say that. 'Forget it.'

'It was the hardest thing I ever did.'

I wasn't sure if knowing that made me feel better or worse. 'It's in the past.'

'Is it? Hayley didn't make it sound that way.'

'Hayley got a little carried away. She's my sister.'

'Whenever I thought of you, which was often,' he said softly, 'I knew you'd be all right because you had her.'

I wanted to touch him so badly. To make sure I didn't, I dug my nails in my palms. Then I put my hands behind my back. My chest thrust forward and I saw his eyes drop to my breasts.

For a moment neither of us moved.

I knew he was thinking about what had happened in the changing room. So was I.

'Do you know what I wish?' I spoke softly. 'I wish we'd just met tonight for the first time.'

'And if we had?' His eyes held mine, slumberous and dark. 'What would you have done?'

'I would have asked you to dance.'

'Maybe I would have asked you first.'

'You wouldn't have noticed me in that crowd.'

There was a long silence. His gaze dropped to my mouth and lingered there. 'I would have noticed you, Ninja.'

We stood there, wrapped in the past and the smells of the city, bathed in the glow that was London at night.

I felt as if my skin were on fire. I was burning.

'Hunter—'

'Was it true what she said?'

We both spoke at the same time and I laughed nervously. 'Was what true?'

'Hayley said you hadn't been involved with another man since me.'

I shrugged. 'No, that's not true. But I learned not to take relationships so seriously. I went out. I had fun.'

'With guys like Brian who wanted you to join a book group and take up baking?'

I laughed. I couldn't help it. Brian was so obviously wrong

for me it wasn't even worth defending myself and Hunter smiled, too, a smile of breathtaking charm, and in that moment I realized that no matter how much time had passed, nothing could dampen the attraction between us. It was off the charts. I'd never had this level of sexual chemistry with anyone, but I knew now it was my problem.

'We'd better go back inside.' I stepped away from him. 'You're supposed to be team building.'

This time around, I was in control of my emotions. My feelings were my problem, not his. It was up to me to handle them. To accept the truth.

He'd been the right guy at the wrong time and I'd always regret that, but it was something I had to learn to deal with.

# 6

IT WAS AN exasperating truth that the harder you tried to avoid someone, the more you saw of them.

I was determined to avoid Hunter as much as possible, so of course I bumped into him everywhere and it was very distracting. To be fair, the rest of the female members of staff were distracted, too.

I tried to work off my frustration in the gym. I took extra sessions and did extra workouts myself.

By Friday of the following week I was physically exhausted but nothing had dampened my sexual frustration.

I texted my sister, 'Pick up batteries on your way home.'

She texted back, 'Pick up Hunter instead.'

I ignored that, gritted my teeth and got on with my day. I avoided the changing room because that made things worse.

I did pretty well until late afternoon when I saw Hunter in one of the studios, hunkered down in front of a skinny boy of about nine. I didn't recognize him.

'He's being bullied at school.' Caroline's voice came from behind me. 'His mum came in earlier in the week and talked to Hunter about whether he should start karate.'

We stood together watching as Hunter talked quietly to the boy and then gave him a lesson, one-to-one.

I could see the confidence flowing from Hunter into the boy, just as it once had with me.

'He's good with kids.' I didn't realize I'd spoken aloud until Caroline agreed with me.

'I guess it has something to do with his own upbringing. It's really important to him to help kids who are in trouble at home. It's kind of like a project for him. Probably because of his own background.'

I tried to remember what I knew about his background and realized it was very little. When we'd been together, we'd been so wrapped up in each other, so focused on ourselves, we'd rarely talked about other things. But as I stared at the tear-stained face of the boy—who was looking a lot happier now—I realized I'd been the same. Older. Probably less endearing. But just as vulnerable.

A project.

I remembered that day Hunter had come over to me and wondered if he'd seen me that way.

Was that why he'd found it so easy to walk away?

Caroline glanced at her watch. 'We're all going out again tonight. There's a new club in Soho. Are you coming?'

I shook my head. I had to try and cure myself and the way to cure myself wasn't to carry on immersing myself in the problem. And anyway, I'd had enough torture for one week.

Instead I put my client through his paces and then decided to find a quiet place to train. I needed to let off steam. We stayed open until ten on a Friday, so I changed quickly and found an empty studio. I didn't bother turning the lights on. Instead I practised kicks.

I'm a black belt in karate—men don't usually want to hear that—but I'd taken up Muay Thai only a few years ago. In

Muay Thai we generally don't kick with the foot. It's full of small bones, easily breakable. We prefer the shin.

There was a bag in the corner of the studio and after warming up, I started practising. The kick is the long-range weapon of Muay Thai and the most important things are speed and placement, so I focused on that.

I thought I was on my own, so when I turned, breathless, and saw Hunter standing there, it was a shock.

'Why aren't you at the club with the others?'

'Why aren't you?'

'I had a client. And I wanted to train.'

'So let's train.' He strolled across to me with that loose-limbed easy gait that made my mouth water and my stomach curl with agonizing tension. As he walked across the room, I noticed he didn't bother turning on the lights. The studio was in semidarkness, the only lights coming from the glow of the city.

And now I was trapped.

I could hardly tell him the reason I hadn't joined them on their night out was that I'd thought he'd be there. I couldn't change my mind without drawing attention to the way I felt. It was my problem.

Dealing with it in the only way I knew, I turned back to the bag but he caught my shoulder.

'No. Full contact.'

In other words, he was giving me permission to kick him.

I wasn't about to object to that.

Thai pad training is a classic way of teaching attack and defence techniques. It helps improve speed, mobility and reaction time.

In theory the pads absorb the blows and minimize the force but I wasn't sure there was enough padding in the world to protect him from the energy I was prepared to put into my strikes. I was handling a lot of pent-up energy.

I waited while he strapped on belly pads intended to absorb punches, knee strikes and kicks and then I started.

I didn't hold back but that didn't seem to bother Hunter.

He stood rock solid as I came at him, coaching me, making suggestions, occasionally demonstrating a better technique.

'You're overrotating on your kicks.'

'I am not.'

'Too much hip turn without the shoulder and arm torque.'

'Anything else?' I turned, fuming and frustrated, and he smiled.

'Yeah, you're cute when you're angry, Ninja.'

The way he said it almost cut me off at the knees.

'Don't call me Ninja.' *And don't call me cute.* The words hovered in the air unsaid and his eyes held mine.

Then he carried on coaching as if that moment had never happened. He gave me some tips he'd picked up in Thailand and I tried not to look impressed even though I was. Training in Thailand was my dream. Secretly I wanted to sit on him and torture him until he told me everything he'd learned but I didn't trust myself to be that close to him.

When I'd exhausted myself kicking the bag, we did clinch work. Close-up training.

Believe me, you did *not* want to be doing that with someone you were trying to avoid.

Without looking at that dark jaw, those powerful shoulders, I slammed him with knees, elbows, and then we were grappling and he tripped me.

*Holy crap.*

I fell onto the mat on my back and he came down on top of me.

I knew from the hold he used that we were no longer practising Muay Thai.

His gaze was fixed on mine and then he lowered his head and kissed me and his kiss was more devastating than anything he could have done with the rest of his body.

There is nothing about this in a Muay Thai training manual. Seriously. Being knocked out just doesn't mean this. He devoured my mouth with his as if I was the best thing he'd ever tasted, as if I were a meal and he couldn't get enough of me. It was as wild as it had been that night in the changing room and somewhere in my blurred brain I realized he'd been holding back when we were together the first time. His tongue slid against mine and I was dizzy with the feel of him, the taste of him, the intoxicating heat of his mouth on mine. My heart pounded at an insane rate and any hope I had of hiding how I felt vanished. I wrapped my arms round his neck but the padding got in the way and I writhed under him, frustrated by the barriers between us.

He shifted his weight so he didn't crush me and then caught my face in his hand so I was forced to look into the fierce blaze of his eyes.

'Is this what you want?' His voice was thickened, his eyes darker than usual and I was so hypnotized by what I saw in those eyes I could hardly breathe, let alone speak.

'Yes. But just sex, nothing else. I'm over you.'

His eyes were dark as flint, hooded, slumberous. 'Right now you're under me, Ninja, which gives me the advantage.'

He had all the advantage, but I wasn't going to tell him that. This time around, I had myself under control. This time, he was the one right on the edge.

The only sound in the room was our breathing. Beyond the glass lay the river and the crush of people that came out to enjoy London at night, but here it was just the two of us.

We were alone, wrapped by excitement and smothered by a sexual tension that threatened to blow my brain.

He eased away from me and hauled me to my feet. Then he reached to help me remove my pads but I stepped back.

I did everything myself now. Everything.

'I'm fine.' My fingers were shaking but I managed it and he watched me the whole time, those eyes dark and assessing, as if he was making up his mind about something. Then he strolled across to the glass and stared down over the river. He leaned his hand against the glass and looked down into the street and I saw the rigid set of his shoulders.

I knew regret when I saw it and this time I was determined to cut him loose. 'Look—maybe you're right. We should just forget it.'

'Is that what you want?' His tone was raw and he turned, his gaze burning into mine. 'Is that really what you want?' He prowled over to me until we were standing toe to toe. My skin felt sensitive and heat uncoiled low in my belly. The look in his eyes made my heart pound because I realized I wasn't seeing regret.

'I—well—' I was stammering, torn between the lie and the truth. I couldn't think with him standing this close. I couldn't breathe. I licked my lips. 'No. I don't want to forget it. I wish…' Oh, God, I was as bad as Brian, stopping in mid-sentence, but Hunter simply slid his fingers under my chin and tilted my face to his.

'What do you wish?'

'Like I said the other night, I wish I'd met you for the first time now.'

'Why?'

I gave a half smile. 'Because we would have had great sex. You're the only man I've ever met who isn't threatened by my turning kick. I don't scare you or threaten your masculinity.'

He lifted his eyebrows. 'That happens?'

'All the time. My turning kick might not impress you but it's a turnoff for some.' I tried to keep it light and suddenly I didn't feel like laughing.

The truth was I longed for someone who liked me the way I was. Who encouraged me and supported me while I travelled the route I'd chosen instead of always trying to push me onto another path.

Hunter wasn't smiling either. He lifted his hand and pushed my hair back from my face. 'I happen to love your turning kick,' he said softly. 'And you don't scare me or threaten my masculinity.'

I suspected that nothing aside from a direct hit in the balls would threaten his masculinity and possibly not even that. I'd never met any man as comfortable in his skin as Hunter.

He was silent for a moment, as if making up his mind about something. Then he muttered something under his breath and let his hand drop.

'So let's pretend we're meeting for the first time. Have dinner with me.'

It was the last thing I'd expected him to say. 'Why would I do that?'

'Because you want to. Because you've thought about me every day for the past five years.'

I gasped. 'You arrogant b—'

'And because I want to, and I've thought about you every day for the past five years.'

His words knocked the protest out of my mouth and the breath from my lungs.

It was like landing on my back on the mat.

I stood drowning in fathoms of emotion, trying to fight my way to the surface, trying to get my head above it so I could breathe.

'It's been a long week. I'm not in the mood for going out.'

'Neither am I. We'll go to my place.' His tone was rough and I immediately knew he was feeling the way I was feeling. I could hear it in his voice.

I stood for a moment staring at the door, knowing I had to make a decision because both of us knew this wasn't about dinner.

We could carry on as we were, dancing around the past, kissing whenever we came too close, fighting it, pretending it wasn't happening. Or we could make an active decision. We could choose to step forward or back.

And I realized Hayley had been right when she'd said I'd never moved on.

I'd never had chemistry with a man as I did with Hunter. And maybe I was seeing the past through rose-tinted glasses, but I knew I had to find out. I couldn't go through life using him as the ruler against which I measured every man—and I was talking figuratively, in case you thought I went round sticking a ruler down men's pants.

I wasn't the same vulnerable teenager he'd rescued. I'd grown up. Last time he'd had my heart, but this time my heart was mine. All that was on offer was my body.

'How far is your place?' I was so desperate I wasn't sure I'd make it and he smiled as he held the door open for me, waiting while I picked up my bag and all my gear.

'One floor. I live upstairs.'

*That close?* My heart rate doubled. 'Upstairs?'

'You didn't know?' He walked down the corridor toward the foyer but instead of going down to the ground floor, we went up. 'I lease the apartment with the rest of the building. It has great views. We can eat and talk without being crushed by the Friday-night London crowd.'

I didn't think talking was what either of us had in mind.

# 7

HUNTER'S APARTMENT WAS spectacular and the crazy thing was I hadn't even known it existed. I'd worked at Fit and Physical since I finished my degree in physiology and sports science and I'd never once wondered what was on the floor above us.

The answer was two floors of real-estate nirvana.

The living room stretched across the whole of the building, open plan with huge glass walls that looked across the river. Cream sofas were grouped around an ultra-modern fireplace enclosed by glass and in one corner was a dining table positioned to make the most of the spectacular views.

'Nice.' I thought of our little apartment in Notting Hill. We loved it but you could barely do a scissor kick without knocking something over. Here you could have held a tournament and still not filled the floor space. 'It's huge. Who are you living with? There's space for the whole of the British karate team.'

He gave a faint smile. 'Just me. I like space. I don't like feeling enclosed.'

'Who lived here before you?'

'A banker. He moved out when I bought the building.'

'So Hollywood pays well.' I strolled to the windows and stared out across the river. 'It reminds me of Nico's apartment.'

'Nico?' His voice was a little cooler and I smiled. I still had my back to him, so I thought the smile was between me and the window but it turned out I wasn't as clever as I thought, because he was standing behind me and the window acted like a mirror. 'You're trying to make me suffer just a little bit for what I did to you.'

'No. I don't play those games.' I could feel the warmth of him behind me and watched as his hands came to my shoulders.

'Who is Nico?'

'He's a lawyer. He's seeing Hayley.'

His grip on my shoulders eased. 'So who was the guy you were with the other night? The one who wants you to join a book group and bake cakes.'

'Brian.'

'What were you doing with him, Rosie?'

'Having dinner.'

'He's so obviously wrong for you.'

I could feel his hands, strong and sure on my shoulders. 'You're not the expert on me.'

'I know you.'

'No.' I turned so that we were face to face, so there could be no mistake. 'You *knew* me. I'm a different person now.'

'Why was he breaking up with you?'

'He finds me scary. Unfeminine.'

Hunter told me what he thought of that in a single succinct word that made me smile and then he slid his hands down my arms and suddenly I wasn't smiling anymore. I felt his palms, warm and calloused, brush against my skin. Knowing what those hands could do, I shivered.

I'd been badly burned, and here I was playing with fire again.

Was I doing the wrong thing?

My courage faltered. 'Maybe I should go. Are we being crazy?'

'No.' His voice was rough and raw. 'I really want you to stay.'

'Why?'

'Because I can't get through my day without thinking about you. Because I can't focus. All I can think of is you, naked and underneath me.' His jaw was tight, clenched, and it was obvious he was suffering as much as I was.

For some reason that made me feel better. Not that I wanted to suffer, but I didn't want to be trapped in this cycle of sexual torment alone.

'Who says I'd be underneath?' I shot him a look. 'Maybe I'd be the one on top.'

His eyes gleamed. 'Maybe you would.'

My breathing was shallow. I still didn't know what was going on in his head. 'I'm not some project.'

His eyes narrowed. 'What's that supposed to mean?'

'Nothing.' I decided this wasn't the time to think about it. It didn't matter anyway.

'I don't blame you for hesitating. I hurt you. I'm sorry for that and I'm sorry I made you wary about men.' There was a raw edge to his tone that caught my attention as much as the hard bite of his fingers and I realized I'd never really thought deeply about his reasons for leaving. I'd been so hurt all I'd thought about was myself.

I looked down at his hand, bronzed and strong, holding me firmly.

We could spend the evening talking about the past, going over what had happened like a tractor with its wheels stuck in muddy ground digging itself ever deeper instead of moving forward. But I knew I didn't want to live my life sinking into the mud of what had happened five years before. I wanted to put it behind me. I couldn't change what had happened, but I could choose not to let it taint my present. I could choose to be in charge of my future.

'It's history.' And finally it felt as if it was. I'd held the dream in my head for so long, held on to the emotions. I hadn't allowed anyone to mention his name, because I'd been so embarrassed by how needy I'd been, but I could see I'd been too hard on myself. Life had felt tough and I'd latched on to the person who had made it easier. Accepting that felt like a step forward.

I felt lighter. Stronger. More in control.

I knew who I was and what I wanted and I wanted him. Not because I felt vulnerable or needed the attention but because he was still the hottest guy I'd ever met and that seemed like a good enough reason to me. And it didn't matter what his reasons were, because I wasn't planning on letting my emotions in on this date.

I suppose we want different things at different times of our lives. At eighteen I'd been desperate for security. *Now?*

His hand tightened on my arm. 'Do you want me to take you home?'

I knew if I said yes, he'd take me to the car, drive me back to Notting Hill and that would be the end of it.

'No. I want you.'

'Are you sure?'

'Yes. But just for sex.'

His eyes darkened. 'Rosie—'

'I just want to be clear about that. I don't want anything else. I don't expect you to prop me up when I feel low, I don't expect you to hold me when I'm sad and I don't expect you to

fight my battles. But we have chemistry—we always have—
and good sex has been thin on the ground.' It had been nonexistent but I wasn't ready to admit that. 'I'm tired of dating
guys I have nothing in common with in the hope we can have
fun in bed. I'll just take the fun in bed and forget the dating.'

Hayley had done the same thing with Nico. Of course, that
hadn't quite turned out the way she'd planned but I wasn't
going to think about that now. I was different. It wouldn't
happen to me. For a start, I was already immune. If you had a
large dose of something, you usually didn't get it again. I'd already caught Hunter. I told myself I couldn't catch him twice.

'Can I use your shower?' I picked up the bag I'd brought
with me and followed his directions.

'Help yourself to towels and anything else you need. I'll
make us something to eat.'

It was a ridiculously intimate exchange for two people who
up until a couple of weeks ago hadn't seen each other for five
years.

I stripped off and stood under the water, aware of the water
flowing over my naked skin. I couldn't stop thinking of him
and I stayed under the water longer than I intended. It felt
symbolic, as if I were washing away the past. When I joined
him in the kitchen, I could see he'd showered, too. His hair
was still wet. His feet were bare.

I was wearing my favourite pair of skinny jeans and a pink
T-shirt. I wasn't dressed up, but neither was he. On the other
hand, Hunter looked good in anything. Hayley was right. He
was gorgeous. Smoking hot, and if I had my way he wasn't
going to be wearing clothes for the rest of the night.

It was time to get Hunter out of my system.

Keen not to look too rabid and desperate, I slid onto a tall
stool while he pulled a bottle out of the fridge.

I'd expected it to be wine but it was champagne and I

jumped slightly as he popped the cork and then watched, fascinated, as he poured it skilfully without spilling a single drop and handed me a glass. His fingers brushed mine and I shivered.

'What are we celebrating?'

'Our first date.' His eyes gleamed and I grinned and raised the glass.

'Sounds good to me. So if this is our first date, you'd better tell me about yourself. Tell me about Thailand.' I sipped and felt the bubbles fizz in my mouth.

Hayley and I only ever drank champagne at Christmas, usually when someone else had brought it, and we usually managed to lose half the contents over the floor when we poured.

It tasted delicious.

'Thailand was both brutal and brilliant.' He cracked eggs into a bowl and whisked them efficiently while I watched.

He told me about his experiences training with the best and if anyone else had been talking, I would have been hanging on to every word because training in Thailand was a dream for me, but I was finding it impossible to concentrate. I tried focusing on his mouth but that didn't work either, because all I could think of was how it felt when we kissed.

I dragged my gaze from his mouth and watched him whisking the eggs. I didn't think that could be erotic, but turned out I was wrong about that, too.

There's something about a man's forearms I find really sexy, especially Hunter's. They were strongly muscled and male. Dark hair dusted skin bronzed by his trip to the Far East. He was powerfully built and supremely fit, every inch of him hard and honed.

As he reached for the salt, I saw the muscles in his shoulders flex. He must have felt me looking at him, because he glanced across and his gaze locked on mine.

He stilled and I tried to look as if I'd been paying attention to every word but I hoped he hadn't been in the middle of asking me a question, because I didn't have a clue what he'd said.

Slowly, he put the salt down.

My heart was pounding like fists against a boxing bag.

We both moved at the same time.

I slid off the stool and he dropped the salt.

We collided in the middle of the kitchen.

I slammed him back and his shoulders crashed hard against the fridge as he ripped at my T-shirt, tearing it over my head.

'Naked,' he growled. 'I need you naked.'

I needed him naked, too, but I was beyond speaking.

His mouth was hungry on mine. His fingers bit into my thighs as he pulled me against him. I could feel the hard, throbbing length of him and his hands were jammed in my hair.

It was rough and crazy. We were locked together and my limbs felt as if they were melting. He lifted me and I wrapped my legs around him. He crossed the kitchen in a couple of strides and lowered me to the counter. My legs were still wrapped around him and I heard the raw rasp of his breathing as he struggled for control.

He stood for a moment, his legs between mine, his hands on my thighs trapping me. Then he lifted his hand and stroked my damp hair back from my face, his fingers lingering on my cheek. For such a powerfully built man, he was incredibly gentle. That probably shouldn't have surprised me, because martial arts is all about control and his control was absolute. And yes, that was sexy. There's nothing as erotic as leashed power and Hunter was all about leashed power.

I could tell he was fighting what he was feeling.

His fingers lingered on my face and he tilted my chin so I was forced to look him in the eyes. My stomach swooped.

I knew this was a turning point.

I knew he'd paused because he wanted me to be sure. He wanted me to have a moment of calm in this stormy, crazy world we created together.

Whether we carried on or not was my choice.

And it was the easiest choice I'd ever made. This moment had been inevitable from the moment he'd walked back into my life.

I lifted my hand and closed my fingers over his wrist, feeling strength and sinew. Then I turned my head and ran my tongue over his palm.

I've no idea what signal he'd been waiting for, but clearly that was enough, because he lifted his other hand, cupped my face and lowered his forehead to mine.

The anticipation was almost killing me.

The ache in my pelvis was so intense I had to struggle not to wriggle on the counter. For several seconds he just looked at me, and I looked at him, wondering how long I could keep this up without ripping his clothes off.

Just when I thought I was going to have to abandon dignity and beg, he slid his hand behind my head and brought his mouth down on mine.

This time there was less of the uncontrolled crazy and more of the deliberate. His kiss was slow, sure and insanely sexy. A strange weakness spread through me, the craving instant and total. If any man knew how to kiss, it was Hunter. I moaned and parted my lips against his, inviting more, offering more. Heat uncoiled deep inside me and spread through my body. My limbs felt shaky and useless. His grip on my face tightened, I felt the erotic slide of his tongue against mine and I lifted my hands to his arms, resting my hands on his rock-hard biceps.

I'd never been with a guy as strong as Hunter. Not that it should make a difference, because it's not as if he used that strength when we were having sex. On the contrary, he controlled it ruthlessly, held himself in check, but there was something about knowing he was doing that that was deeply sexy. He was all man, from the top of his glossy hair to the soles of his bare feet.

He curved an arm round my back, holding me firmly, and the other slid to my breast.

I wasn't wearing a bra, because frankly, there wasn't much point. The rough pads of his fingers grazed my nipple and sensation shot through me. Just a touch, a simple touch, and yet already I was desperate. The pleasure was dark and exciting, the intensity just a little scary.

He kept his mouth on mine, explored my mouth with ruthless control, but I could feel that control slipping. I could feel the change in him, feel the ravenous hunger that made his kiss a little rougher, a little harder and I didn't mind, because I felt the same way. Something happened when we were together. Something that, for me, had never happened with anyone else.

Without lifting his mouth from mine he dropped his hands to the counter either side of me, caging me. I could feel him through the thick fabric of his jeans, rock-hard and ready. I heard myself moan and slid my hands round his back and under his shirt. My hands made contact with sleek male skin and rippling muscle. I ground myself into him, heard him curse softly and then he was lifting me off the counter and unzipping my jeans. It took a couple of attempts because his hands weren't quite steady and my jeans were glued to me but somehow that made it all the more exciting. I sensed that he was right on the edge of control and I loved the fact it wasn't just me who felt this way. And then I was naked, my jeans on the floor with the rest of my clothes, and he lifted me back onto the kitchen counter. I gasped as the cool surface touched my bare bottom. I was wondering what he had in mind when he straddled the stool in front of me. His eyes were dark, hooded and fixed on me. Holding my thighs apart with his hands, he finally broke eye contact and lowered his mouth to my inner thigh.

The contrast between the cold of the surface and the heat of his mouth made me moan. I felt his tongue trace the sensitive skin at the top of my thigh. Everything he did was full of explicit promise and my insides reached melting point in two seconds flat. I needed him inside me, right then, but he didn't seem in a hurry to oblige. Instead he proceeded to torture me with pleasure. He explored every single part of me except that one place that was desperate for his touch.

'Hunter...' I moaned his name, thinking that I might have to kill him if he didn't put me out of my misery soon.

His tongue trailed maddeningly close to that part of me and I tried to shift my hips but his hands clamped tight on my thighs, holding me trapped and still so that I was totally at his mercy.

'Please—please...' It was more of a moan than coherent speech but he must have got the message, because finally I felt his fingers part me, felt his tongue dip inside me, caressing with unerring accuracy and wicked skill until I was almost sobbing with the sheer overload of pleasure. I was so close, *so close,* my hunger for him wild and out of control, but he held me on the edge of it, refusing to give me what I needed.

Through the pounding of blood in my ears I heard the scrape of the stool on the tiled floor as he stood up, a crash as it fell, but neither of us took any notice. I don't think we would have noticed if the roof had fallen in, because the only thing that mattered to us right there and then was what we were doing to each other.

His mouth was on mine and he was kissing me with raw, sensual demand. Finally he let go of my hips, but only so that he could pull a condom out of his pocket. I tried to help, but that simply slowed things down and I heard him curse softly as he gently pushed my fumbling fingers out of the way and dealt with it himself.

His mouth was still on mine and he sank his hands beneath me, hauled me off the counter so that my legs were wrapped around his waist and sank into me with a deep thrust. I dug my nails hard into the thick muscle of his shoulders. I'd forgotten how big he was and just for a moment I wondered how this was all going to work, but I was so wet, so ready for him, it was as if we'd been designed to fit perfectly together. My body tightened around his and he groaned deep in his throat, an earthy primal sound that told me everything I needed to know about the way he was feeling. And I was feeling the same way. I couldn't breathe. I was drowning in sensation, knowing I'd never, ever felt like this before, not even the first time we were together.

He just stayed without moving and I could feel the thickness of him, the strength and power deep inside me. I rested my forehead against his and our eyes held. That connection was every bit as intimate as the merging of our bodies. I had no idea how he was managing to hold back, because I was ready to explode. I discovered that anticipation could be painful. That needing someone could drive me almost to screaming pitch. And then he withdrew and thrust deep again and after that, control ceased to exist for either of us. He filled me, drove into me, dominated me, until the world outside ceased to exist and the only thing that mattered was what we shared. His mouth was hot and skilled, each forceful thrust of his body sending me closer and closer to ecstasy. Sex between us had always been good but never, ever had it been like this. We climaxed together, the pleasure a relentless, overpowering rush that consumed us both and left us fighting for air.

*Holy crap.*

My arms were locked around his shoulders, now slick with sweat, and I felt the scrape of stubble as he dragged his mouth from mine and kissed my neck, his breathing rough and uneven.

I closed my eyes, trying to find my sense of balance.

A faint flicker of unease rippled beneath the soporific pleasure that followed the storm.

I'd told myself this was just sex. But there was no 'just' anything when I was with Hunter. Everything was intense and exaggerated and the whole lethal mix of the man and my feelings threatened more than my equilibrium.

I heard him inhale.

'That was…' He stopped midway through the sentence, only I knew in his case it was because he was struggling.

'Yeah.'

'How long since—?'

'None of your business.'

I waited for him to say something but he didn't. I waited for him to put me down, but he didn't do that either. Instead he eased away from me, but only so that he could shift my position slightly and grab the champagne and glasses—with one hand. Don't try this at home. Then he carried me out of the kitchen.

It was a bit caveman.

Still wrapped around him, I pressed my mouth to his face. 'You Tarzan, me Jane.'

'Hi, Jane. Want to get naked with me?'

'I think we already did that bit. Where are we going?'

'I'm going to show you my loincloth.'

We were both laughing but even laughter didn't lessen the sexual high, and then we were in his bedroom and he set me down on the bed, which was a relief because my legs felt so weak I wasn't sure they'd hold me if he'd expected me to stand.

Somehow he managed to put the champagne and the glasses down without spilling anything and turned to face me.

'This time,' he said slowly, 'we're going to do it properly.'

I wondered what he thought we'd just done.

# 8

HIS BEDROOM FACED over the river and I could see the London Eye in the distance. I imagined all the tourists in those glass pods training their binoculars on the Houses of Parliament and Buckingham Palace and catching sight of Hunter naked in his apartment. He was more impressive than any London landmark—but he didn't offer two-for-one tickets, so you can forget any ideas about increasing visitor numbers.

I sat on his bed, naked apart from the pink T-shirt, and he was still dressed.

I believed in equality. 'Take your clothes off.'

That made him smile. 'I hoped you might do it for me.'

'That works for me. What did you mean when you said we were going to do it properly?'

He topped up our glasses. 'We're going to take our time. We have five years to catch up on, Ninja.'

Despite all my protests, the name made my insides melt.

It was personal.

It was ours.

Something of the past that locked us together and made

this more than a mindless sexual encounter. Nothing could change the fact we had history.

He handed me a glass and I sat up on his bed and took it. I'm not much of a drinker generally, because I'm so serious about training. It didn't take more than a few gulps before I could feel a warmth slowly spreading through my limbs. Or maybe it was being close to him.

Keeping his eyes on me, he dragged off his shirt.

My gaze slid upward to his shoulders, power-packed muscle. He'd always had a good body, but the years and intense training had added definition.

His jeans were undone at the waist and a line of dark hair guided the eye downward.

My mouth was dry and I took a mouthful of champagne and then put the glass down and shifted across the bed so I was eye level with the thick ridge of his erection, which was as big as the rest of him.

Looking up at him, I slid my hands round the bare skin of his back and then pushed his jeans past his hips and down his legs.

Hunter had been my first and they say you always remember your first, but even if he hadn't been, he wasn't a man any woman was likely to forget.

He was perfect to look at and I devoured him greedily with my eyes before leaning forward and taking the whole hot, hard, smooth length of him into my mouth.

His breathing changed and it gave me a feeling of satisfaction to know I affected him as deeply as he affected me.

I took my time. Exploring him with the tip of my tongue, taking him deep, teasing him until he groaned and sank his hands into my hair. I felt the hard bite of his fingers against my scalp and then he eased away from me, flattened me to the bed and came down on top of me.

'I want you again.' His voice was thickened, his eyes dark and dangerous as he held my gaze.

'I want you, too.'

He kissed his way along my cheek to my mouth and I felt the rough scrape of his jaw against my skin. My stomach tensed with anticipation. I didn't understand how I could want him again so badly after what we'd just done.

He slid his hands to my hips and flipped me over. I felt his hand slide down my spine, linger on the curve of my bottom and then slide between my thighs and I closed my eyes because he knew exactly where to touch me, exactly how to drive me wild.

He pulled me up so that I was on my knees, anchored my hips with his hands and slid deep. I closed my eyes. I couldn't see him but my erotic imagination soared into overdrive. I could visualize how we must look, him with those powerful thighs pressed hard up against mine so there was no space between us. Me, my hair tumbling forward over my face, my bottom lifted to him as I knelt before him like some pagan sacrifice. He drew back and then thrust again and I moaned, feeling every inch of him. I was so aroused, so sensitized, the pleasure close to agonizing. My neck was damp with sweat, my whole body trembling with every deliberate thrust. I knew I wasn't going to last. He knew it, too, but this time it seemed he wasn't going to make me wait. Or maybe he was the one who didn't want to wait, because he reached forward and slid those skilled, expert fingers over my slick flesh. The first ripple of my orgasm drew a groan from deep in his throat. I felt myself tighten around him and then my loss of control became his and he erupted in a forceful climax, holding me tightly as he buried himself deep. It was primal, primitive and nothing like anything we'd shared before.

Afterward I didn't think I was capable of moving. I felt

wrung out, shattered and a bit stunned but he eased away from me, rolled me over and came down on top of me, his gaze fixed on mine with disturbing intensity.

I stared up at him, trying to look cool about the whole thing, but I felt as if I'd suffered a direct hit from a meteorite. I couldn't move, couldn't think, so when he reached across and pulled another condom out of the drawer by his bed, I gave a whimper of protest.

'Hunter, I can't. I'm too sensitive. You can't possibly be able to— Oh…'

He slid his hand under me and this time he entered me slowly, by degrees, taking his time, proving once again that his self-control was so much better developed than mine, and I discovered I wasn't too sensitive. I discovered that sex with Hunter was an addiction I wasn't likely to recover from any-time soon.

I wrapped my legs around him, slid my hands up his chest and stroked my hands over the hard bulge of his biceps.

The excitement was almost unbearable and I knew he felt it, too, because he kept his eyes on mine the whole time, which made the whole experience more intimate. There was no way either of us could not know who we were with. He was as into me as I was him. Our mouths fused, his tongue stroked mine and he thrust deeper. Dimly, in the back of my mind, I realized I was in trouble. I was supposed to be get-ting him out of my system. I was supposed to be detached and just interested in sex, but this felt like so much more than that. I tried to grab hold of that thought and work out just how much trouble I was in, but his hand cupped my face as he surged into me again and again, adjusting the angle until the whole of me was flooded with intense white heat. With every skilled stroke, he proved just how well he knew me and I moaned his name, losing all hope of playing it cool or hiding my feelings. He was so strong, so masculine in every way and everything we did was on a different level.

I felt myself tighten around him, heard him swear under his breath as my body gripped his and we both lost control at the same moment. I held on to his broad shoulders, battered by the powerful surge of pleasure, swamped by a wash of sensation that threatened to drown me. He lowered his mouth to mine and we kissed right through it so that there wasn't a single part of us that wasn't involved and engaged.

*Total sex,* I thought. I'd given all of me. Everything.

*Everything except my heart.*

We stayed like that for a long time, his weight crushing me, my arms holding on to him. Then he seemed to realize he was probably too heavy and he rolled onto his back and took me with him so I was curved against him. His arm kept me locked against his side. My head rested on his shoulder, which basically meant I was staring at his chest. Women probably would have bought tickets to see this view.

His arm tightened. 'I missed you.'

It was the last thing I expected him to say and I closed my eyes tightly, trying to push back the emotions that threatened to engulf me.

'Really? Because I hardly noticed you were gone.'

'So Hayley was lying when she said you cried every night for six months?'

I sensed from his tone he was smiling. 'She was exaggerating. She always exaggerates.'

'No, she doesn't. She's a scientist. She bases everything on fact. She said you lost weight.'

'That was intentional. I was training hard.'

There was a brief pause. His grip on me tightened. 'I'm sorry I made you cry, Ninja.'

'I'm not. If it hadn't been for you, I never would have dated men like Brian and think what I would have missed.' I made light of it because the alternative was getting heavy and I didn't want that, but when I tried to sit up he held me tightly.

'I hurt you.'

'I don't really want to talk about this.'

'Why?'

'Because if we talk about it, I have to remember my awful behaviour.'

He rolled onto his side and looked at me, a frown on his face. 'Awful?'

'I was so needy. I smothered you.'

'You were having a difficult time.' He stroked my hair back from my face. 'How are things with your parents now?'

'Okay. We don't see that much of them. I have Hayley and we have a great group of friends. I suppose our friends are our family. I'm sorry for my parents.' It had taken a long time to feel that way, but it was true. 'They were so wrong for each other. They just made each other miserable.'

'And they made you miserable.'

I shrugged. 'Plenty of people are fucked up by their families.'

'That's true.'

I realized I didn't know much about his family. He'd told me once that his mother had left when he was young and that he'd lived with his father. It had all sounded pretty normal to me, but most things were compared to my crazy, dysfunctional family. I realized now that my own altered perspective had stopped me asking more questions. 'Were you?'

His grip tightened. 'I was fine.'

That wasn't enough for me. I wanted to know more. Last time we'd been together I'd been focused on my own issues, but now I'd moved on and I wanted to know about him. 'Was that why you spent so much time at the gym? Because home was grim?' At the time I hadn't even questioned it. I'd been so focused on myself and my own problems I hadn't thought to question why he'd spent so much time at the gym. I'd presumed it was because martial arts were his passion.

He rolled onto his back and sat up. 'Do you want some food?'

I wasn't really listening.

I was remembering what he'd said on that first day, about everyone having something in their lives. At the time I'd been so swamped in my own misery I hadn't picked up on it.

'I want you to talk to me.'

'I need something to eat.' Without looking at me, he pulled on his jeans and strolled out of the room to the kitchen and I sensed he wasn't walking away because he was hungry.

I realized now that when we'd been together, I'd been the one to do all the talking.

I slid out of bed, too, pulled on my shirt and followed him into the kitchen.

'When we were together, you never talked about yourself.'

Without looking at me, he turned the heat up under the pan. 'You had enough worries of your own. And anyway, talking doesn't help.'

'It did for me.'

'Good. It's important to know what works.'

'I want to talk about you for a change.'

He didn't turn. 'Talking doesn't change the facts.'

'But knowing the facts can sometimes help someone understand.'

'What do you want to understand?'

In my head there was a vision of him squatting down in front of the little boy in the gym. Hunter Black, who had trained stars in Hollywood, giving all his attention to a child who was being bullied.

'Tell me about your family.' I pushed my hair away from my face, conscious that wild sex had left it tangled and messy. 'I mean, do they even know you're back? Have you told them?'

'There's no one to tell. My mother lives in Spain now.'

'What about your dad? You once told me your dad was the reason you took up karate.'

'He was. Indirectly.' He picked up the eggs he'd abandoned earlier. 'Omelette all right with you?'

'Fine, thanks. What do you mean, "indirectly"?'

There was a long pause and then a sizzle as the eggs hit the pan. 'He hit my mother. She sent me to karate so I would be able to defend myself if something happened to her. She saved what little money he let her have and spent it on lessons for me.' He paused. 'I went because I wanted to be able to defend her, which was a pretty big ambition for someone of that age.'

'Oh my God.'

It wasn't what I'd expected him to say.

I stared at his broad bare shoulders, not knowing how to respond. Remembering how protective he'd been of me, it was all too easy to imagine he would have been the same with his mother. 'How old were you?'

He tilted the pan. 'Four.'

My heart tightened. 'You were *four* when he hit you?'

'No, I was four when I started karate. I don't remember when he first hit me but I do remember my mother pushing me into a cupboard to protect me and locking the door.'

My heart was pounding. The horror of it engulfed me like a grey, dirty wave. 'She did that?'

'She hid the key so he couldn't get me, but he knocked her out and they took her to hospital without realizing I was in the cupboard.' He reached for two plates and divided the omelette, as if we were talking about our plans for the summer, not something that had formed him.

'How long were you in there?'

'They kept her in the hospital overnight.'

I thought of him, four years old and trapped in the dark. I remembered what he'd said about not liking enclosed spaces and suddenly his choice of apartment made sense. Not just because it was above the business but because it was a collision of light and space. No one could ever feel trapped here. 'What happened? Did your mother leave him?'

'Eventually. Not soon enough. I was eleven. It wasn't easy for her. She'd had a rough life and she saw him as security. He used that to manipulate her. He made her feel as if she wouldn't be able to survive without him. In the end being without him was the only way she could survive.' He handed me a plate and I took it without even looking at the food.

'And she left you with him?'

'She made the right choice. It was about survival.'

'Were you angry with her for leaving you?'

'No. I was relieved. The responsibility was crushing. It had got to the point where I was afraid to leave her alone in the house with him. It meant I only had myself to worry about.'

I tried to imagine how that must have felt, being a young boy and feeling responsible for the safety of your mother.

I looked at him. The food on my plate remained untouched.

I realized how little I'd known about him. How little I'd asked.

'Where is your dad now?'

'He died a few years ago. Cirrhosis, which was a surprise to no one given that his longest relationship was with the contents of a whisky bottle.'

'And your mum?'

'She's safe. And happy. She met somcone.' His voice softened and I felt something squeeze inside me.

I wondered how he'd handled it so well.

He added a chunk of fresh bread to his plate but I shook my head when he offered me the same.

'No, thanks.'

'You need carbs.'

'I'm not hungry.' What he'd told me had taken away my appetite. 'You never told me any of this.'

'It was history by the time I met you.'

But it explained why he'd always seemed so strong and self-reliant. He'd had to be.

We took the plates back to bed and finished the food and the champagne.

I looked at my phone and realized it was 2 a.m. 'It's late. I should go.'

'Stay the night.' His tone was rough and I looked at him, sorely tempted.

Hayley wasn't home. She'd texted me earlier to say she was staying at Nico's for the weekend. Also that she was borrowing my favourite shoes because she was accompanying him to some smart lawyer do.

There was no reason to go and plenty of reasons to stay. Like the way Hunter was looking at me and the slow, seductive brush of his fingers over my arm. My skin was super sensitive, my insides melting.

It wasn't as if we'd exactly denied ourselves. There was no reason to feel this desperate, but still I was desperate.

I'd always thought my willpower was pretty good. I could resist chocolate and biscuits, but it turned out I couldn't resist Hunter.

He was my weakness.

'I don't have anything with me.'

'I have everything you're likely to need.'

That was what worried me.

I pushed that thought aside and slid out of bed. Then I

picked up the plates and took them to the kitchen, telling myself that it was fine to stay. That I could cope with it. That my emotions were under control.

If you want to justify something, it's pretty much always possible if you work hard at it. But the only real justification as far as I was concerned was that I wanted to.

I was having the best time of my life.

*Why not?*

# 9

'COFFEE?'

I woke to find sun streaming through the windows and Hunter standing next to me, a towel knotted around his hips, his hair wet from the shower.

Groaning, I sat up and pushed my hair away from my face. 'You were up early.'

'It's ten o'clock.' He handed me the coffee. 'Not that early.'

'Ten? You're kidding.' I reached for my phone, saw that he was telling the truth and felt heat rise in my cheeks. 'I was tired.'

'I think I might know the reason for that.' His tone was a soft masculine purr that made me want to ditch the coffee and drag him back into bed.

My muscles ached in places they hadn't ached for ages. Thanks to him, I was aware of every part of my body.

I sipped my coffee and then put it down on the table next to the bed, feeling suddenly awkward. After last time, I was determined not to do anything that could be defined as clinging. 'I should get going. I expect you have plans.'

'My plans include you.'

I probably should have played it very cool and made some excuse about needing to be at home, but as I opened my mouth to speak, I turned my head and the words jammed in my throat. The towel had slipped slightly, revealing even more of the hard, honed abs and the powerful muscles of his chest and arms.

I told myself that any woman who would be able to walk away from that needed therapy.

'What did you have in mind?'

He gave a slow smile and I smiled, too, because it was obvious how we were going to spend the weekend.

I reached out and tugged at the towel, but he was already coming down on top of me, pulling the covers back, exposing me.

I slept naked, so there wasn't much chance of hiding, not that I wanted to.

Sunshine fell across the bed, spotlighting my body and his. He lowered his head, plundering my lips and then moving lower. He took his time, driving me mad, tormenting me with every skilled flick of his tongue. He didn't just know how to kiss my mouth; he knew how to kiss all of me and he employed those skills with devastating effect on my breasts and then lower to the damp, swollen heart of me. The pleasure spread through me in hot waves and he teased and tormented me until I was writhing on the bed and then he locked his hands on my hips and forced me to lie still while he took his time and explored me with merciless skill. My body was his playground and by the time he pulled me under him I was almost sobbing with desperation.

He paused for a moment, looking down at me, and then he sank into me, driving deep into the heart of me with unleashed hunger. If he'd held back last time, he certainly didn't this time. My hands moved to his shoulders and I felt the ripple of muscle under my fingers, felt the hard strength of him as he pulled back and then drove deep. My hands slid lower and closed over the hard bulge of his biceps. His eyes held mine and he lowered his forehead to mine and then kissed me, biting at my lips, nibbling and driving me crazy while all the time his body possessed mine.

I was consumed by sensation and so was he. Excitement spiralled around us, drawing us closer, spinning a web that locked us together.

He dominated me, drove into me with a relentless perfect rhythm until we both hit the same peak at the same time and exploded together in an overload of pleasure.

The wildness of it shocked me and I think it shocked him a bit, too, because he rolled onto his back and folded me into his arms and held me there until both of us could breathe properly again.

'Why didn't you stay in Hollywood?' I lay there filled with questions, wanting to uncover every secret, every hidden corner of him that I didn't already know.

'I enjoy coaching. Hollywood was a means to an end. I earned enough to be able to buy this place.'

'And a cool car.'

'That, too.'

I asked him again about Thailand. He asked me about everything I'd been doing. We had a huge gap in our history and we filled it in together, learning, discovering. We were filling in the blanks. Joining the dots.

We lay in bed, made love and talked. We talked about things we'd never talked about when we were together the first time. I didn't even check my phone, because I was absorbed and time wasn't relevant.

We spent the whole weekend in bed.

He rang for takeout food and walked downstairs to the door to collect it, but apart from that we didn't leave his apartment.

The hunger in him matched mine.

I might have missed the fact it was Sunday night had a text not come through from Hayley. 'I forgot to buy batteries but as I haven't heard from you, I guess you don't need them. :)'

I was about to switch my phone off when another text came. 'Be careful.'

I knew she wasn't talking about the sex. She was talking about my heart.

And I realized I'd put myself at risk again. 'Just sex' didn't mean spending an entire weekend with a guy, talking about every subject under the sun. It wasn't getting to know him and wanting to know all the small things. But that was how I felt with Hunter. I wanted to know every corner of him. I wasn't interested in superficial; I wanted depth.

I just couldn't help myself around him. I couldn't stop myself falling.

Hunter was watching me, sensing the change. 'Are you all right, Ninja?'

The endearment cracked me wide open and I realized in a rush of panic that I'd been kidding myself. This wasn't just sex. With Hunter it never had been and it probably never could be.

I'd thought that if our relationship was just about sex, I couldn't be hurt but when my heart was involved? That was different. That made me vulnerable.

I wouldn't allow it to happen to me again.

I had to protect myself.

'I have to go.' I shot out of bed without looking at him and rummaged for my clothes. 'Hayley is at home.'

'She's not a kid.' His voice was soft. 'She doesn't need a babysitter.'

And I realized then that there was no point in being anything but honest, so I turned, clutching my shirt against me.

'I can't do this, Hunter. I thought I could, but I can't.'

He was very still. 'Which bit can't you do?'

*Love,* I thought silently. *I can't do love.* Not when it was one-sided. Not when all the feelings were mine.

'This. Us. It's going to make our working relationship awkward. People are already noticing and talking about us.'

'Let them talk.'

'It isn't a good idea to sleep with the boss.'

'I'm the boss and it seems like a good idea to me.'

Whatever I said, he countered, pressing closer and closer to the truth, but I'd learned my lesson. This time around, my feelings were my problem, not his. I wasn't going to dump them all over him again, as I had the first time.

'Well, I'm the employee and it's awkward for me. This has been fun, but it was a one-time thing. Just the weekend. From tomorrow we're back to being how we were.'

'And how were we?'

'Colleagues. I don't want to be intimate.' But I realized that we'd never been anything but intimate, and with that admission came the unpalatable realization that I was probably going to have to leave my job because I was never, ever going to feel normal around this man. I wasn't capable of feeling indifferent. 'Just colleagues.'

He gave me a long steady look. 'Are you sure that's what you want?'

'I'm sure.' I made for the door before he could see through the lies. Last time I'd smothered him in my feelings. This time I was going to spare him that. 'I'll see you at work tomorrow.'

I limped through the next few weeks, pretending I was fine. Every minute was torture. I gritted my teeth and counted down the hours until the weekend, when I didn't have to see him.

Three weeks after I'd done the 'let's be colleagues' speech, I was lying in bed with the duvet over my head pretending to be asleep when I heard my sister open the door.

Hayley wasn't fooled. We'd shared a room growing up, so she always knew when I was asleep and when I was faking.

I felt the bed dip as she sat down.

'I have coffee, an untouched packet of chocolate biscuits or a glass of wine. You pick.'

I didn't answer. I hoped she'd go away, but of course, this was my sister, so there was no hope of that. Instead the duvet was tugged from my fingers and she wriggled into the bed and snuggled under the covers with me.

'Do you want to talk about it?'

I would have thought the duvet over my head would have answered that question, but Hayley wasn't easy to deflect. 'I'm fine.'

'Right. Because not eating, sleeping or laughing is totally you, as is spending an entire Saturday in bed.'

I wanted to say something flippant but my throat was clogged with misery. I hadn't allowed myself to cry, but suddenly I was crying and my sister was holding me and she was muttering 'Shh' and 'I'm going to kill the bastard' as she stroked my hair.

'Not his fault. My fault for loving the wrong man.' I choked out the words but it didn't stop her listing all the dire methods of torture she had in mind for Hunter Black.

'You're crazy about him. You always have been.'

And suddenly I was telling her everything. How it had been at work, about that weekend, all of it. 'When I'm with him, I can be myself. I never feel as if I'm being judged. He likes me the way I am. He doesn't want me to join a book group or learn to bake cupcakes. He doesn't care that I have a flat chest or that I like practising my kicks while we're talking.' I scrubbed my face with my hand and sat upright. My head throbbed from crying. 'And he makes me laugh.'

My sister looked at my swollen face and raised her eyebrows. 'You're not laughing now.'

'That's not his fault.'

'Have you told him how you feel?'

'After last time?' I grabbed a tissue and blew my nose. 'No way.'

'Maybe he feels the same way you do.'

'No. For him it was just about fun and sex. That's how I wanted it to be, too!' I shredded the tissue. 'I'm going to have to leave my job.'

'You love working there!'

'Not anymore. It's too hard. Too awkward and I don't want to embarrass him a second time. I'm going to look for something else. And I know that makes me pathetic, but—'

'It doesn't make you pathetic.' Her phone beeped to indicate a text but she ignored it. 'You need to leave this bed and come out with us tonight.'

I managed a smile. 'Just because I can't get my own sex life sorted out, doesn't mean I want to ruin yours. Go. Nico is texting you.' I gave her a push. 'Go and have fun. You can borrow my shoes if you like. I don't need them.'

I couldn't imagine ever wanting to go out again.

She slid out of the bed and paused in the doorway. 'I still think you should tell Hunter how you feel.'

'This time around, it's my problem. I'll handle it.'

But handling it drained me.

Every time I saw him approaching, I dived for cover and I stayed later and later to avoid leaving at the same time as him, but he left late, too, because he was the boss.

I stopped going to staff nights out, then decided not going made it look as if I was avoiding him, so I went and pretended to have fun on the dance floor. I concentrated so hard on 'having fun' I almost sprained my ankle.

Proving I was fine was exhausting. My smile muscles were getting a more rigorous workout than my abs or my thighs.

And then finally I heard I had an interview at a fitness club closer to home.

I should have been thrilled. Provided I didn't mess up the interview, this nightmare would be over. And then I realized taking this job would mean I wouldn't see Hunter again. He really would be out of my life.

And that was the biggest nightmare of all.

'What are you doing for your birthday, Rosie?' Caroline stuffed her bag into the locker and pulled out her water bottle.

'I'm having a quiet night.' I was going to hide under the duvet and hope that when I woke up a year older, I'd be cured of the way I was feeling.

But my sister was having none of it.

'You are not spending another Saturday night in bed watching TV. That's not happening. I've planned you a surprise party.'

'I really don't—'

'Shut up and get dressed in something warm. Wear that gorgeous coat you bought last winter. The short, sexy black one that makes you look like a Russian princess.' She was checking her phone. 'We need to go. Cab's outside.'

For my sister's sake I washed my hair and dragged on my clothes. The black coat was a perfect contrast to my white face. I felt like crap and I looked like crap. I knew I needed to snap out of it. I was no fun to be with. And it was no one's fault but my own. I'd played with fire. I'd been burned. Again.

Hayley bundled me into the cab and handed the driver our destination on a piece of paper so I couldn't see.

'Don't you think you're taking this a bit far? I've lived in London all my life. I'll know where we're going.'

'No, you won't.' She pulled a scarf out of her bag and tied it around my eyes while I protested.

'Oh for…' I thought it was overkill. 'You'll smudge my makeup.'

'I want it to be a surprise.'

'The surprise is going to be me looking as if I'm dressed for Halloween. Who is coming, anyway?'

'Our friends.' It was a suspiciously vague answer and I was starting to feel exhausted when she tugged off the scarf.

'We're here.'

And in spite of everything, I smiled, because we were right next to the London Eye, my favourite place.

'You booked a night flight? That's perfect.' I could see our friends gathered waiting and I felt a warmth spread through me. It was the closest I'd come to feeling happy since I'd broken it off with Hunter.

I still had my sister. I still had friends. I'd got over him before. I'd get over him again.

I could learn to live without breath-stealing excitement. I could afford extra batteries.

We tumbled out of the cab and our friends swarmed around us. I was handed lots of interesting parcels and bags that my sister took away and tucked in a larger bag she'd brought with her.

'You can have them later.'

'What's wrong with now? I can open them during the flight.'

'You should be looking at the view and concentrating on the stuff that matters. Like my gift to you. It's waiting in the capsule.' She leaned forward and hugged me. 'Happy birth-day, Rosie. I hope it's a special one.'

'Why have you left my gift in the capsule? Someone might steal it. What is it?'

She pulled away from me and gave me a long look, a smile and then a little push. 'Go on, birthday girl. Find out.'

Still looking at my sister, wondering what she'd bought me, I climbed the steps. I was expecting her to follow but she just stood there in the middle of our friends, watching with a smile on her face. I knew something was going on but I had no idea what.

Only when I stepped into the capsule did I turn my head. Hunter stood there, with his back to the view, watching me. 'Happy birthday, Ninja.'

# 10

I STARED AT him, felt a flicker of panic and then turned quickly to find my sister and the others but the attendant was sealing our capsule and the rest of my group were on the other side of the barrier, watching avidly.

My eyes met Hayley's accusingly and she blew me a kiss.

I'd assumed my present was a trip on the London Eye, but I realized now her gift was Hunter. We were about to spend thirty minutes suspended over the city in our own private glass bubble. Just the two of us. Thirty minutes during which I had to hide how I felt about him. It was going to be the longest thirty minutes of my life.

It was probably going to be the longest thirty minutes of his life, too.

I felt awkward.

He'd obviously been manipulated into it by my sister, but he probably thought I was behind it because it was just the sort of stunt I would have pulled at eighteen if I'd had the funds. 'I'm sorry. I knew nothing about this. You should have said no.'

'Do you wish I had?'

I gave a casual shrug. 'I love having friends around me

on my birthday, but I'm sure there are a million other places you'd rather be. This was Hayley's idea.' I wanted to smile, but honestly, my face was exhausted. I had no idea why fake smiling was so much more tiring than real smiling but it was. I just couldn't do it anymore.

'No, it wasn't. It was my idea.'

The capsule was slowly rising upward but I wasn't looking at the view; I was looking at him. 'Yours?'

'I know how much you love the London Eye. I thought it was time we talked.'

'I see you every day at work.' I was going to kill Hayley for agreeing, but I wasn't going to be able to kill her until the capsule had finished its circle, which meant that for the next half an hour I was locked in an enclosed space with Hunter.

'You've been avoiding me.'

'I've been busy.'

'But now you're not busy, so you can listen to what I have to say.'

'Sure.' I shrugged and strolled to the glass, pretending to look at the view. I kept my back to him. Easier to control my body language that way.

It bothered me that just occupying the same space as him could have this effect on me.

The capsule rose slowly and I could see London spread out beneath our feet. Lights flickered across the dark surface of the river. It would have been captivating if I hadn't been a captive. I saw his reflection in the glass and knew he was standing right behind me.

'I want to talk about why I left.'

'I already know. I was clingy.'

'That isn't why.' He curved his hands over my shoulders and I wished there were an emergency exit or something, because the last thing I wanted or needed was to think about that time in my life. I'd die of embarrassment and I was pretty sure it wasn't going to be good for tourism having a corpse in this capsule.

'We don't need to talk about this. I don't blame you. I understand.'

'No, you don't understand.' His tone was raw and his hands tightened on my shoulders. 'I didn't leave because I didn't care. You didn't drive me away. I left because I knew it was the right thing to do. But leaving was the hardest thing I've ever done.'

I stood still. 'It was hard?'

'I was crazy about you.'

My stomach curled. I felt a wild flutter of excitement that I killed instantly. 'That makes no sense.'

'When we met, you were vulnerable. Lonely and, yes, pretty messed up. I wasn't sure of your feelings.' He breathed deeply. 'You were emotionally raw. Would you have wanted to be with me if that hadn't been the case?'

I wondered how he could possibly have come to that conclusion. 'I was crazy about you, too. We spent every minute together.'

'Exactly.' He paused, his mouth tight. 'And I didn't want that responsibility. It didn't feel right to me. It was too close to what my mother did. And yes, I was scared. I was afraid of letting you down, of failing you.'

'So you went to Thailand?'

'There were plenty of other places I could have trained, Rosie.' He turned me gently so I was forced to look at him. 'Why do you think I picked Thailand?'

'Because you wanted to get as far away from me as possible.'

He gave a humourless laugh. 'You're so wrong about that.'

'You always wanted to train in Thailand.'

'Train, yes. Not move there.' His tone was raw. 'I did it

because I loved you and I wasn't good for you. I left because I knew if I didn't, we'd start it up again.'

My knees were shaking. 'You loved me?'

'You know I did.'

'No, I didn't know! You never said.'

'Maybe not those exact words, but I thought it was obvious. Do you remember your eighteenth birthday?'

'Vaguely.' I saw him smile and I couldn't help it—I smiled, too. *Crap.* I was hopeless at playing it cool. 'Oh, all right, yes, I remember it. Mostly because you drove too fast.' And because he'd made it special. Every kiss, every stroke, every gentle touch, had made sure my first time would be the best. The way he'd held my head as he'd kissed me, taken his slow, thorough time to take our relationship to the next level. 'We had sex. It was no big deal.' It had been the biggest deal of my life.

'Everything changed. Our relationship was so serious, so intense. You were so afraid to go and live your life. Instead you clung to the safe option, the familiar.'

'Now we're getting to the embarrassing bit,' I muttered, but he simply smiled and scooped my face into his hands. What I saw in his eyes made me dizzy. 'I don't blame you for going to Thailand, although it was a long way to go to avoid me.'

'I wasn't avoiding you. I didn't trust myself. I knew if you were there, under my nose, I'd want you back. I knew what I wanted.' His voice was raw. 'It was you I wasn't sure of. I wasn't sure you knew what you wanted and then you started giving things up for me and that made my decision.'

'What about my decision?' Anger flickered. 'You could have said all this and I could have told you what I thought. And anyway, you're talking rubbish. I didn't give anything up.'

'You gave up your college place so that you could stay with me.'

I felt my cheeks heat. 'I wasn't that bothered about college.'

'And now you have a degree in physiology and sports science. Would you have had that if I'd stayed?'

I swallowed. 'Probably not. After you left, I gave up on men and surrounded myself with friends. I lived my life, dated guys like Brian. Guys who were nothing like you.'

There was a brief pause. 'And how did that work out?'

I could have lied, but I didn't see the point. 'Pretty crap. Most men don't like me practising my turning kicks on a date.'

'I'm sorry about the way I did it. I'm sorry I hurt you.'

He'd torn me off him like a piece of sticky tape—quickly. I saw now it had been the right thing to do.

'That's the past.' I used the words he'd used to me all those years before and I could see in his eyes he remembered.

'Good. Because I want us to start again. And I want to know how you feel about me.'

I thought about my dreams, the images that rolled around my head tormenting me when I was supposed to be sleeping. 'My feelings are my problem.' My voice was soft, although goodness knows why, because we were suspended above the river Thames and no one could hear us. 'I'll deal with them.'

'Tell me.'

I gripped the rail and stared down at London sparkling beneath us. It felt surreal. It felt as if we were on a magic carpet, flying over the city. 'We've always had something special….' I kept my eyes forward, not looking at him, because I was trying to be measured and not gush all over him. 'Sex is part of that, yes, but for me there's more. I can't just switch off everything else and you don't want that. You don't want someone loving you and I understand that after what you saw with your mother.'

'What my mother shared with my father wasn't love. It was

an unbalanced, inequitable relationship with all the control on my father's side.' His voice hardened. 'He sapped her of confidence until she believed she couldn't exist without him. That's not how we are.'

'We?'

He slid his hand behind my neck and I felt his fingers, strong and warm against the nape. 'I want all of it, Ninja.' His voice was low and sexy. 'I want the good and the bad, the exciting and the mundane. I want to prop you up when you feel low, hold you when you're sad and fight your battles.'

He was throwing my own words back at me and I stood for a moment, mesmerized by the look in his eyes.

'I learned how to do those things for myself.' I was trembling. 'I fight my own battles. I comfort myself when I'm low. I have a secret stash of chocolate for that purpose.'

The corners of his mouth flickered. 'Being able to do those things for yourself doesn't stop someone else doing them alongside you. I don't just want sex, Rosie. I love you.'

My knees were shaking. He'd called me Rosie, not Ninja. He'd said— 'You love me? But when—how—when—?' Oh, God, now I was doing it. Not finishing my sentences.

'"When" is easy to answer. I fell in love with you when you climbed on the back of my motorbike. I tried to get you out of my system. Maybe I did for a while, but when I saw you in the restaurant that night, I knew my feelings were as strong as ever. As for the why—' he gave a half smile '—how long have you got?'

My heart was pumping. 'How long do you need?'

He glanced out of the capsule and judged the time left before we arrived back at the beginning. 'I'll give you the highlights. I love your sense of humour. I love the way you laugh so hard you can't stop yourself. I love the fact that you can knock me over with a kick if you get your balance right—'

'There's nothing wrong with my balance!'

He slid his arms around me and hauled me hard against him. 'I love how much you love your sister and your friends. I love—'

'Stop!' Feeling as if I were flying, I covered his lips with my fingers and then lifted myself on tiptoe and wrapped my arms round his neck. 'Stop talking and kiss me. I really want you to kiss me because it's magical up here and I want to have this moment to remember always.'

He lowered his head to mine and he kissed me while the world outside sparkled, the lights of London a carpet beneath our feet and the stars above like jewels in a sky of velvet-black. I'd never been this happy, ever. I knew that there were no guarantees. No one knows the future. But right now this was what I wanted. And I wanted it for all the right reasons.

I didn't want Hunter for security; I wanted him for himself. 'I love you, too.' I whispered the words against his mouth and felt him smile against my lips.

When I eventually pulled away, something made me glance down toward the capsule beneath us and I saw my sister and the rest of our friends gazing up at us, grinning like idiots. I could see they were holding a birthday cake and gesturing.

'They're going to eat my cake. I will kill them.' I'd never loved my sister more than I did at that moment.

I was so happy I did a turning kick in the middle of the capsule and almost smacked Hunter in the head.

Amused, he pulled me back into his arms. 'Happy birthday, Ninja.'

'Thank you.' I slid my arms round him, my present. *My gift*. 'This was the best birthday.'

'It isn't over yet. This is just the beginning.'

As he brought his mouth down on mine, I closed my eyes, thinking that if this was the beginning, then the future was looking even better than my birthday cake.

★ ★ ★ ★ ★